The Whole Man

THE WHOLE MAN

Aude

TORONTO

Exile Editions
2000

This edition is published by Exile Editions Limited,
20 Dale Avenue, Toronto, Ontario, Canada   M4W 1K4

Sales Distribution:
McArthur & Company
c/o Harper Collins
1995 Markham Road
Toronto, ON
M1B 5M8
toll free:
1 800 387 0117
(fax) 1 800 668 5788

Design by *Michael P. Callaghan*
Compostion by *Tim Hanna*
Typeset at *Moons of Jupiter, Inc.* (Toronto)
Cover Painting/Interior Paintings by *Mladen Srbinovic*
Printed by *AGMV Marquis*

ONTARIO ARTS
COUNCIL

CONSEIL DES ARTS
DE L'ONTARIO

The Canada Council | Le Conseil des Arts
for the arts | du Canada
since 1957 | depuis 1957

The publisher wishes to acknowledge
the assistance toward publication of
the Canada Council and the Ontario Arts Council.

ISBN 1-55096-537-9

To all the fathers and mothers,
who are also children,
who also have fathers and mothers,
who were fathers and mothers themselves,
who had parents, who …

Part One

We are databases
of insignificant details,
of resoled memories.
The body is an opinionated scriptor.

— LAURIER VEILLEUX
Précipité de la mémoire

CHAPTER 1

Simon wakes up with a start, he has the taste of metal in his mouth as though he had just removed the barrel of a gun. Saliva dribbles down his chin. He wipes it with the sheet.

Last Thursday, at five o'clock in the morning, he located his carotid artery with his finger and pressed the tip of the blade against it until a bit of blood pearled at his neck. He had been told that was how *samurai*'s wives killed themselves to escape from capture or dishonour. They sliced the jugular vein with a pretty little dagger given to them by their husbands that they carried with them everywhere. Simon only broke the skin, but he felt as though he could go further one day if he decided to. He preferred the image of the woman's suicide, the *jigai*, rather than the horrifying *suppuku* of the *samurai*. Knife in hand, he stood immobile for a long time before the big windows that looked out over the trees of the fog-enshrouded Aoyama cemetery.

It's always in the faint light of dawn, when Simon hasn't received any e-mail during the night, that such thoughts assail him.

He set up his computer on a table with wheels over three weeks ago so that he can put it wherever he likes in the big studio. He leaves it on, even when he goes out. That way, when he returns he can tell right away if he has received a message.

When he lies down, he puts the table on the right side of the bed, right next to him. When he wakes up, he opens his eyes, lifts his head slightly, and he knows.

It is four twenty-three in the morning, and he knows. He won't receive anything from Chloé again tonight.

Words surge into his mouth and spill over his lips in a hushed voice, like vomit.

Without getting up, Simon gropes around the floor for the bottle and drinks straight from it. The whiskey burns his stomach instantly and fills him with bitterness. He grimaces.

He plunges onto the bed and stays there, rigid, waiting to drop back into absence. Eyes open, he stares at the ceiling and calculates complex figures without purpose to avoid thinking.

Then suddenly, he turns sharply to the right, throws one last glance at the screen, drops his head onto the mattress, and curls up so tightly it seems as though he is trying to swallow himself up. But he is immediately wracked with sobs.

Simon sits back up, tears the sheet away and leaps out of bed.

Naked, he measures the studio by counting his steps. After each of his night-walking episodes, he records the number of steps he took in a notebook. At the end of the night, he adds them up. He keeps track of the degree of his insomnia this way, even when he goes out for a walk in the neighbourhood.

The air is humid and warm. Drizzle begins to wet the windows. In the distance, the neon inscriptions along the tops of the buildings are merely spots of colour that transform the landscape into a Borduas painting.

This is the third rainy season Simon has lived in Tōkyō. One complete month of deluge, absolute humidity, mould everywhere, sticky surfaces, crinkling papers and books, exaggerated odours and permanently sweaty bodies.

In mid-July the rains stop, but everything stays damp in the intense heat, which draws a light haze from the ground and surrounds every thing and being with a halo of fine vapour.

Simon is already suffocating. He walks back and forth, gazing toward the glass walls where everything begins to cloud and dilute before his very eyes.

He sits on the bed again, quickly jots down the number of his steps in the notebook on the bedside table. Then he walks over to the computer and composes a brief message to Chloé. He sends it right away, then pushes the table away and starts pacing again.

She won't answer his message. She doesn't answer his messages. Even on the telephone. He had already left many messages on her voice mail in vain. He doesn't do that anymore. And he sends her a few words by Internet less and less often, because he feels as though he's wasting his time. Writing to Chloé is now like writing fiction. When he is at his worst, he even believes that he has invented this woman. These are the times he takes out the two pictures of her that he has brought with him.

In the first one, Chloé is sitting on the rail of the balcony of her house in the country. She has slipped her feet between the bars and is swinging, which makes her face and upper body slightly blurry. Her hair is swinging as well and she is bursting with laughter.

In the second photo, she is lying asleep in the grass. They had walked for several hours in the forest and made love in a small clearing. Chloé had fallen asleep and Simon had tried to take her picture close up, without her knowing, in an attempt to capture the solemnity that her face conveyed the first night he met her.

He had never managed to understand this woman. And now, she has become completely emphemeral.

When he arrived here over two years ago, they wrote every day on the Internet. They often replied to one another immediately. Between messages there was just a slight delay akin to the time chess players take to evaluate the situation and carefully plan their strategy before making their move. There had been something of that in their exchange. As though, even at opposite poles, they were unable to put an end to the turbulent, obstinate discussions that they had gotten stuck in over the last few years — and which had contributed to Simon's departure.

Over time, they had exhausted one another with their sterile exchanges and their messages got further and further apart. The tension between them was eventually lost, but at the same time, so was the intensity and intimacy that had brought them to life. They became more and more anecdotal and banal.

They maintained this pretense of an exchange for several weeks. And then it evolved normally, smoothly, into silence.

Then, months later, without any explanation, Chloé started sending very short messages, only at night: "Talk to me!" "Please!" "Where are you?" "I don't hear from you any more." "Why aren't you telling me anything?"

Surprised, Simon worried at first. He started to write her again, but she didn't seem to receive his messages.

He concluded that there was some technical problem and had his computer and Internet connection checked. But his messages still didn't seem to be reaching their destination.

He tried to reach Chloé by telephone, but got her voice mail every time and, despite the messages he left her, she never called him back.

It wasn't until she wrote, "Who are you?" that he understood this was something completely different, Chloé's new strategy. She wanted to bring Simon onto a wavelength he had never dared go with her.

Irritated, he ordered her to stop her game. But the messages continued to reach him, enigmatic and disturbing — in one direction — as though Chloé was lost in space and calling her last cries for help to him, all the while drifting irretrievably further and further away.

One morning, when Simon got up and went to his computer, which was still on his desk at the time, there was no message. Nor was there in the days to follow.

The game had ended.

Simon had been waiting for this moment for a long time. Yet, instead of being delighted, he felt totally abandoned.

For weeks, he received nothing from Chloé, who seemed to have perished, body and possessions, somewhere, sucked into a black hole.

After a while, contrary to all logic, Simon tried to contact her by sending terse messages in turn: "What has happened to you?" "Are you ill?" "Why don't you answer?" "What exactly is this game you're playing?" "What do you want from me?" Several times a night, he left a message on her voice mail.

One day, he asked one of his associates from Montréal to go to Chloé's and see her.

When Simon learned that she was all right, but that she refused to have any contact with him, his worry soon cantered into rage.

Simon kept quiet, and decided to break things off for good.

Despite his decision, he did not shut down his computer once during the weeks that followed, in case Chloé had changed her mind. And he was unable to resist the desire to glance at the screen when he passed.

Then one night Simon received the first two pages of a narrative that, it seemed, had nothing to do with him or Chloé. The text had a title, "Protective Seals," and it finished in the middle of a sentence. It seemed like the beginning of a novel that took place in Montréal around 1920. The characters were an importer, Monsieur Drouin, and his young clerk, Gérard.

The message was sent by Chloé, but it seemed as though she must have made a mistake when selecting the recipient from her address book. She had a friend who was a writer and sometimes sent his texts for her to read and comment on.

But during the nights to come, Simon received more pages and he quickly understood the story, which was in fact like the beginning of a novel, but concerned him personally: it told the story of his father Gérard.

This made no sense at all. Simon had never spoken of his father to Chloé.

Even stranger was that each new page added details to the story that even Simon did not know. He only recognized the general outline of the text. His father had never talked very much and Simon knew almost nothing of his past.

In fact, Gérard had only really told his son about himself in the last hours of his life.

And as his dying father spoke to him, Simon had been counting and re-counting the tiles on the floor of the room. He had not listened.

CHAPTER 2

Protective Seals

When he was sixteen, Gérard began working as a clerk for Monsieur Drouin, an independent travelling salesman who had conferred on himself the grand-sounding title of Health Product Importer.

The merchandise he offered his clientele was limited to three products he supposedly imported directly from Europe, for which he was the sole distributor in Québec.

His cough syrup and vitamins did in fact arrive from France by boat. The *Coupetoux* was so pungent and strong that when swallowed it invariably induced a coughing fit which, according to Monsieur Drouin, was certainly purgative. As for the *Vitavi* vitamins, they were virtually as miraculous as making a novena to the good Saint Anne.

His third product, *Suisseau*, was supposed to be one of the most reputable waters from a region in the Swiss Alps. It was actually sulphurous spring water secretly bottled by his brother in Joliette.

The importer had set up headquarters behind his Montréal home on Boulevard Saint-Joseph, in a large warehouse that served as both storage depot and office. From the outside, the building didn't seem like much, but on the inside it was perfectly comfortable, insulated, and heated by a coal-burning stove that sat in the centre of the room. As you entered from the street, crates were stacked carefully on the right side. On the left, a large desk covered by a thick layer of paper gave the impression that great things were happening here. Behind the desk, an imposing oak cupboard provided a storage place for the most important and confidential documents. It was locked. Nearby, there was a comfortable English easy chair, a *torchère* lamp and a pile of magazines and newspapers sitting on the rug that provided an ideal spot to relax.

What Monsieur Drouin enjoyed the most about his work was the direct contact with people. This often led him to travel across the city "to seduce his clientele," as his wife liked to say (not without a touch of irony). She had borrowed the expression from her husband who, when he was in full form at Christmas and Easter dinners, would try to explain to his lovely twenty-year-old niece that sales was the art of seducing a clientele rather than presenting a logical argument. There was no doubt about it in Madame Drouin's mind when she watched her husband, all dapper and dashing, leave to go on his rounds.

Monsieur Drouin got along very well in business on his own. He didn't need an employee, but during a particularly laborious delivery to a brothel in the lower town, his back seized. It was lucky for him that there was a charlatan nearby.

During the weeks to follow, Madame Drouin applied hot plasters to his lower back. In spite of her efforts, his back was still so weak that he was incapable of moving the smallest crate. He could no longer go pick up his merchandise in the port or Joliette and put it in his warehouse. Nor could he deliver it. On each delivery, he had to transport the cases to and from his van. To make matters worse, much of his clientele, mostly women, lived on the second or third floor. And these women didn't order one or two bottles of cough syrup, spring water or vitamins every now and then; they ordered entire cases. They were usually in charge of ordering for their neighbours, relatives and friends because each time Monsieur Drouin opened a new sector, he always kicked things off with a "cooking demonstration."

Gérard had grown up at his Aunt Germaine's, three blocks from the Drouins. His mother Gisèle had died during his birth and he didn't have any brothers or sisters. His father, Rodolphe, left to work in the lumber camps when his wife died. Gérard was afraid of him. Every time he visited, Rodolphe got drunk and always ended up getting so angry with his son — who was still a child — that his aunt had to intervene. His aunt barely loved him either, though he was a good, useful boy. Germaine had "picked up this miserable orphan," as she liked to say, but she resented him without declaring it openly, for the same reasons as Rodolphe. As though Gérard had killed Gisèle on purpose when he was born.

Gérard often did odd jobs at the Drouins. By age thirteen, he had repainted the fence and the little wrought-iron gate in front of their house, among other things. Monsieur Drouin had a way of offering a "contract" to him that made Gérard feel like an adult, almost an equal. Once he had made the terms of his business proposition clear, including a precise definition of the work to be done, the quality he wanted and the price he was offering, Monsieur Drouin would invite Gérard to "talk business." The first few times Gérard couldn't muster a counter-offer, but Monsieur Drouin forced him to, threatening to give the work to someone else. These negotiations were of no risk to Monsieur Drouin because his initial offers — completely unreasonable — were made up with the phoney negotiation in mind.

Gérard, on the other hand, felt that Monsieur Drouin respected him as a person, at least much more than his father did, and conferred boundless admiration upon him. Without really noticing he was often duped when the work was being assessed. When he had repainted the wrought-iron gate and fence, for example, they were thoroughly rusted. Before he was able to apply the paint, he had to brush and scrape them vigorously, which was not in the "contract." To make matters worse, they were full of curls and interlink, which made the job long and difficult if Gérard was to avoid dripping paint as Madame Drouin insisted.

For years, Gérard had also done little favours for Madame Drouin, most of the time without Monsieur Drouin's knowing.

She had a veritable passion for the fruit jellies made by a small confectioner on the other side of town. Even though he went there often for business, Monsieur Drouin had long refused to bring her any because he could not stand to see her feast with such obvious pleasure on the sweets. In his mind, a woman as level-headed as his wife exhibiting such surprising passion must be hiding other delights that he would very much like to experience with her — but she never gave him a glimpse. He was willing to give her a fur coat, a crocodile handbag, pay a cleaning woman to come in every week, and take her on a trip to the United States every summer, but not the little insipid, sugary things that gave her more pleasure than any person could. It was a question of honour.

For Gérard, the trip to the confectioner's meant riding the tram for a good hour, though he was certainly compensated upon his return. Of course, Madame Drouin paid him for his trouble, but what really made Gérard happy was to see Madame Drouin's face light up when he secretly gave her the precious package.

In the beginning, Monsieur Drouin had found the near constant presence of his employee in his business difficult. But he needed him in the warehouse and during his deliveries. Once Gérard brought the merchandise to his client, Monsieur Drouin often asked him to go wait in the delivery truck so that they could settle up in private.

What Gérard enjoyed the most were the cooking demonstrations that Monsieur Drouin occasionally allowed him to attend. Monsieur Drouin would spend an hour giving a high-spirited performance for about twelve women who were dolled up as though they were going for a drink down at the hotel — you would have thought the circus was in town. His demonstrations were so popular that he didn't even have to publicize the opening of a new sector. One of the women who attended from another neighbourhood always ended up inviting him to give his promotion at her place.

Over the years, Monsieur Drouin had perfected his sales pitch to such an extent that, as Gérard observed with fascination, the women practically fell under his spell in less than fifteen minutes. Most of Monsieur Drouin's sales chat had nothing to do with his products, and everything to do with the individuals in his audience, because he had truly mastered the art of making them believe that he had noticed each of them personally and chosen them individually from the crowd.

And what he said about his dubious products was just as fabulous. The sulphurous and bad-smelling water that surged from the bowels of Joliette supposedly came from a crystalline rain that fell on the summit of the highest mountain in Switzerland. This water, already so pure that it could have performed miracles in and of itself, had taken decades to come down the mountain, pass through many natural filters — the underground layers of sand as white as snow, the patches of edelweiss, the kilometres of spongy moss that couldn't be found elsewhere. At each stage, the water acquired properties capable of regenerating each cell of the body so it could maintain or regain its vigour and youth.

Monsieur Drouin had more than his fair share of imagination, culture and vocabulary. Gérard couldn't get over it. Not only did he drink in his boss's words, but from time to time he stashed a bottle of the miraculous water. He still did not know its exact origin even though he went to Joliette to receive the delivery of the cases of *Suisseau*.

His boss had told him that the water arrived by boat in Boston from Europe, and was then shipped to his brother Jérôme's by airplane. In fact, there was a short landing strip hidden in a field behind one of Jérôme Drouin's buildings. Gérard, who had never seen an airplane up close, asked if he could come and watch as the plane landed. Monsieur Drouin explained to him that only he and Jérôme could attend the delivery. No one could know who supplied the *Suisseau* if Monsieur Drouin was to maintain a monopoly on the sales of this product that represented the majority of his income. Gérard swallowed the lie and with it, in his eyes, the water gained added value.

Several months later, Gérard learned that *Suisseau* had more hidden secrets. He discovered this one morning when, fairly tired from a wild time the night before, he wanted to regenerate his cells with a drink of *Suisseau* in the warehouse. The water tasted so bad because of its curative properties that Gérard had taken to drinking it in one gulp with his eyes closed. Just as he was getting ready to swallow, he choked on something even more miraculous than what he was expecting to pass through his throat — it was a mouthful of high-proof moonshine.

CHAPTER 3

This morning, between night and dawn, the Tōkyō sky passes only from one shade of grey to a lighter one.

Simon didn't receive any mail, yet again. It's been more than ten days since the narrative stopped mid-chapter. And now, Simon needs to know the rest of the story.

In the beginning, Simon was mostly intrigued by "Protective Seals." He sought in vain for a logical explanation of why someone might be sending him this novel of sorts from Chloé's address — a novel in which his father was the protagonist. Simon also tried to figure out whether it was a piece of fiction, woven around a few real facts, or a true account of Gérard's life. For the moment, he tended to believe, because of the last pages, that it was some twisted version of the truth, written to portray his father in a more favourable light.

The image of Gérard as it was in the story actually had very little in common with the terribly harsh one that Simon knew. Perhaps that was why Simon had read the first chapters with a certain distance. That is, until his mother Estelle appeared in the narrative as a young woman who, in her undescribable beauty, looked like Vermeer's *Girl with a Pearl Earring*.

From that moment on, Simon anxiously awaited the next parts. Especially since he had only received "Protective Seals" in bits and pieces, sometimes just a few lines at night, until the last paragraph he received over a week ago, which led him to believe that Gérard was madly in love with Estelle.

Exhausted, Simon drags himself to bed. After writing the length of his sleepless night in his notebook, he falls into a profound, empty sleep, from which he is torn at six-thirty by his alarm.

Simon stands motionless in front of the bathroom mirror for a while. His skin is sallow and his face has lost all brightness. As though his thinning body has slightly given way over these last months.

Simon doesn't like the image projected back at him. It makes him angry. He exercises several times during the week in the building's exercise room and, until recently, his body rarely showed signs of fatigue, even when he had jet lag. Simon seemed to have escaped the slow, ravaging erosion time seemed to inflict on men often younger than he was.

He starts to shave with the unpleasant impression that the face in the mirror is not exactly his own.

In the shower, he turns a cold spray of water on his body and shudders. He finally wrenches out of his torpor. He shakes off the water and snaps at his body with a small damp towel. Then he vigorously towels and rubs himself dry with the bath sheet.

He makes an espresso and drinks it while reading his agenda. He is so distracted. He thinks about which suit to put on from the wardrobe. What he wears has taken on considerable importance lately. Simon has always liked being well dressed, but his penchant had become something completely different of late. As though he expected some kind of magic from the clothes of the great couturiers, almost a proof of identity. Perhaps because he felt as though he didn't have one anymore.

This wasn't linked solely to the fact that, here, every man is inevitably lost, dissolved and drowned in the monstrous anonymous crowds of corporate men in dark suits who invaded the train stations, streets and buildings of Tōkyō daily like swarms of grasshoppers coming from every direction.

For several weeks now, every time Simon puts on a suit by Jean-Claude Poitras or Yves Saint-Laurent, it's as though he has a fresh hope of being someone by proxy, unable to become what he once was, full of confidence and determination.

Simon had never experienced insomnia before everything started to insidiously come undone inside him. He would sleep like a log, without dreaming or tossing and turning from midnight until dawn, his digestion and colour never upset by worry or drink — ever.

He had studied marketing because he loved to coolly observe everything that happened around him, the subtle movements, the slightest degrees of impetus that determine the trends of society.

Simon had mastered the art of intuiting what needed to be created, developed and offered to consumers, at any given moment, the fleeting illusion of what would finally be able to fill the void, the questions without answers, the unsatisfied wants and even the insatiable desire for a god.

"Protective Seals" had come to disrupt Simon's nights and his work showed it. But the real disruption had begun a long time ago, with Chloé.

Simon had never lived with the woman and he had never thought, until very recently, that this link could have so profoundly shaken his life.

He would rather not believe it, rather link the crisis he was going through to the fact that he was starting his third year in Tōkyō, this strange and abysmal city in a constant state of movement, and with which it was difficult to establish a clear and stable rapport. Through patient exploration, he felt that he had begun to make her his, and then suddenly she would get away on him again. And the things he thought he loved about her, he had started to hate.

When he agreed to come to Tōkyō for three years, he had already been several times for work. So full of alluring paradox, the megalopolis awoke his curiosity and set his imagination ablaze. He was fascinated by the simmering congruence of such disparate, discordant worlds, knocking against one another on the surface, while below, the tectonic plates of the Philippines, Eurasia, and the Pacific meet in a constant, earthquaking battle.

The first year, Simon lived a certain rapture, nearing exaltation. Although, he felt vaguely that his state of mind had not only been provoked by the discovery of this fascinating city, but also by the fact that he had managed to tear himself away from Chloé. As though he had fled just before some terrible misfortune. He couldn't quite say what, but it threatened everything that he was and everything that he had built until now. He was certain of it. And even though they were fiercely pursuing their deaf exchange from a distance, Simon felt safe on his far-off island.

When his time wasn't monopolized by management taking him to see the major attractions and, occasionally, the more secret ones of the city, he liked to explore the local neighbourhoods alone, adventuring off to the infinite maze of streets that was hidden behind the massive, crowded major routes and formed a mosaic of amazing little villages. He almost always got lost and had to use city maps, which he showed to passersby as he came across them, to find his way. His last resort was to look for the little neighbourhood police station where he first held out his *meishi*, his business card, bowing forward. Once the police officers had learned his identity and, more importantly, the firm for which Simon worked as a consultant, they took pleasure, with gestures and drawings, to show him the way, if they did not simply accompany him to an area that was more familiar. During these long moments adrift, he had made a thousand and one enthralling discoveries.

The next year, when the rainy season returned to bog everything down, his enchantment ended, almost suddenly. Simon still loved the city, but now his relationship with her was more realistic and reasonable. The frenzy of their first contacts had calmed down.

From that moment on, Simon had expanded his field of exploration to all of Japan. For months, as soon as he had a few days free, he would leave on the *Shinkansen*, a fast train, or by plane, to discover new regions, sometimes so diverse that it was impossible to imagine they belonged to the same country.

Now, he never feels like going anywhere because of this story and his mother who has just appeared in it. As though that was the only thing that mattered to him.

He doesn't feel good in Tōkyō anymore. Something indescribable is preventing him from really being there. Yet he isn't anywhere else. He's living in *no man's land*.

The firm that hired him has rented a large studio for him, at the top of an entirely Western building in Minami-Aoyama, a neighbourhood where many foreigners live. Everything there looks just as it might be in any of the larger North American cities.

Simon feels like his life is happening inside a giant snare. *Trompe l'oeil.* A cardboard decor behind which something is resisting, hiding, irretrievably.

Now as soon as his work is done, he takes refuge most of the time in his studio where he eats a few bites in silence. He buys cold boxes, prepared near the train station, that are divided into small compartments, *bento*, containing *norimaki*, dried fish, pieces of *tōfu* in *miso*, mouthfuls of sticky rice, pickled plum, and other simple food items. He shuts himself in his apartment and doesn't emerge until the next morning, except to go for a walk at night in the nearby streets.

He has a hard time accepting that this city is becoming unbearable to him. Several foreigners have told him that this is normal, even after living here for a few years, even after really feeling settled. It'll last a few months, they told him. Then everything will gradually become strangely familiar, without him really noticing, even the language — the lilt of it will imperceptibly graft itself onto his. And one day, he will feel more like a foreigner at home than here.

Simon won't have the time to go through all these stages. He is going home in eight months. Between now and then, he would like to make amends with this city he now loathes.

The glass tower where he works is in Shinjuku, one of the most overflowing and noisiest parts of Tōkyō. Last week, when he had gone out to dine alone, to escape for a short hour and a half from the swarm of engineers who had been buzzing around him all morning, he stopped short in the middle of a sidewalk, suddenly suffocating in the crowd, milling like a gigantic nest of worms.

The humidity was oppressive and odours lodged in his throat. But it was above all the deafening noise that assailed Simon and overcame him, to the point of making him nauseous.

Traffic was at a complete standstill because men at work with jackhammers were forcing the compact mass of pedestrians to step briefly off the sidewalk and spill over into the roadway, which was met by a flood of impatient honking. Some music managed to thunder out of a *pachinko* hall to Simon's left, through the rattling of thousands of metallic balls pumping through the narrow passages of hundreds of pinball machines crammed into the room. Each shop spat its publicity out into the street through booming megaphones. On the side of a building, a baseball game was projected onto an immense screen. A helicopter spewed out political propaganda from overhead.

Simon was unable to move, completely lost, causing an abrupt eddy in the current. He lowered his head and vomited on the sidewalk. He wondered where he was.

CHAPTER 4

Monsieur Drouin and his brother Jérôme had been born under a lucky star. All their lives, they were able to sniff out the sweet deal in a sea of disastrous business possibilities. For example, when a fire de-stroyed part of the the Saint-Henri district, they improvised as building con-tractors, and even went as far as to say that the business had been passed down to them from their father.

Their father worked more in demolition than construction, if you took what he did to mean covertly setting fire to well-insured buildings. Actually, he had been found one morning, charred, behind a restaurant to which he had just set fire. The police believed that it was an unfortunate mishap.

Monsieur Drouin sought advantage on every occasion, right down to adapting his discourse to his clientele. So during the war, when anx-iety was written across everyone's faces, his vitamins became calming for the nerves if the dose was doubled and sleeping pills if it was tripled. And of course you could always count on *Suisseau Réserve Spécial* to take away your sorrows and fears, to help you forget for a moment all the atrocities that were happening in the old countries. It was in fact a very popular remedy. The only difference between this vintage and the regular *Suisseau* was a tiny little bulldog head, stamped on the bottom of the bottle. It was Jérôme's trademark — a sign of the golden business he was doing with the Americans.

The Spanish flu had also caused a spectacular increase in Monsieur Drouin's sales. His cough syrup, a little too bitter to be appreciated before, was now guaranteed to kill all dangerous germs on the spot. Monsieur Drouin even advised a discreet rinsing of your mouth after kissing someone. Paired with the rotgut *Suisseau*, this syrup had joined the ranks of prophylactic measures to purify the system and prevent all contamination.

Another factor influencing the success of Monsieur Drouin's business was prohibition, which had been imposed in Québec and Canada, and also in the United States.

When Gérard learned that his boss was smuggling contraband alcohol, manufactured by his brother, it didn't bother him in the least. On the contrary. He spoke openly about it to Monsieur Drouin, who decided to make Gérard take an oath on the spot and took the same opportunity to offer him a raise. Gérard instantly became a sort of moral associate to Monsieur Drouin. Of course, his salary had not been increased by much, but Gérard had the impression that he had attained a certain status in the company, in knowing the great secrets of the trade.

And the next week, when they went to Joliette to get the merchandise, Gérard found out that Jérôme knew he had got a whiff of what was going on. Before, when Gérard would bring the cases of *Suisseau* to the truck, Jérôme sent wary glances in his direction and was always off talking to his brother. This time, Jérôme slapped Gérard on the back and invited him into his office for three gulps of what Gérard thought was the famous home vintage, though it was actually a much finer, fruity *eau-de-vie*, which he was unable to identify but instantly regretted having swallowed in one gulp.

Encouraged by his promotion, Gérard put a lot more heart into his job and even started to make certain deliveries alone, to clients with whom Monsieur Drouin had less affinity. There had never been any open discussion of Monsieur Drouin's individual clients, or about the long and frequent visits to the brothels in the lower town, where he made major deliveries of the *Suisseau Réserve Spécial*. Gérard tacitly knew that he had taken the oath so that he never made mention of any of these things in front of Madame Drouin. Gérard never would have done it anyway, to avoid hurting her.

The little sweets shop on the other side of town had closed its doors long ago, but Gérard still secretly ran a few errands for Madame Drouin. He had grown attached to the woman and would have liked very much to have her for a mother.

Business was booming, and more and more often there was an air of joy in the warehouse. Some days when they came back after their rounds, Monsieur Drouin invited Gérard for a drink and then back home for dinner.

Even though it only happened once or twice a week at first, Madame Drouin started to cook more, preparing recipes that she had not made for years and making sure that there was always enough for three. Over the months, Gérard ended up having dinner at the Drouin's every night, even on holidays.

Monsieur Drouin usually closed up shop in June and July to take "Blanche to the States," as he liked to say. She had family in Maine. After the customary visit was paid to her relatives, they went to the sea where they stayed in the best boarding houses.

Now that he had an employee, Monsieur Drouin no longer had to close down the company while he was away, so he decided to entrust his business to Gérard during his vacation. Gérard only had a few deliveries of *Suisseau Réserve Spécial* to make while he was away. The rest was on hold until his boss returned.

Even better, Monsieur Drouin left him to look after their house. Gérard moved in for two months; it was a nice change from the dark little room he had been renting for some time in a *pension* where the odour of boiled cabbage and meat on hooks hung in the air.

Upon his return in August, Monsieur Drouin declared that it would be more convenient for Gérard to stay on. In the days that followed, he moved into a larger, sunnier room from the one he had stayed all summer, the one the Drouins called the guest room — even though no guests ever came.

That night in the warehouse, Monsieur Drouin, who had had more to drink than usual, revealed to Gérard in no more than three sentences that the room had belonged to their only son, who had died of a burst appendix when he was eight. They hadn't had any other children because Madame Drouin had fallen ill after the birth of Julien and had had "the big operation."

Gérard never learned anything more about it, but he understood how meaningful the room the Drouins had offered him really was. For the first time in his life, he felt as though he was part of a real family. He barely slept the first night, he was so happy.

Soon, the big house livened up again. They played cards and board games after supper. Monsieur Drouin didn't stay late in the warehouse anymore, under the pretext of having to do the books or take inventory.

He even went back to teasing his wife, as he hadn't done for years, kissing and flirting with her in poorly concealed advances that she could only turn down for appearance's sake, while Gérard looked on in amusement.

Chapter 5

Every morning, except Saturday and Sunday, at seven-thirty sharp, a taxi driver in white gloves waits for Simon at the door of his building. Originally, there were three passengers. But the American had finished the eight-month internship at the company he came to work for and went back home. The Irish fellow, however, had gone to live in the Moto-Yoyogi district where several other Irish lived. Their departures had comforted Simon.

He had always liked silence in the morning. But Brian, the Irishman, could talk forever. He had even taken to knocking on Simon's door in the morning so that they could go down to the lobby together. In the halls and the elevator, he would tell him about the latest adventures he had had the day before, in this "mad and crazy world" where everything seemed to surprise and amuse him to the highest degree.

When they arrived downstairs, Tom, the American, would be waiting for them, smoking, slumped in one of the easy chairs in the lobby. Tōkyō seemed to make this boy from a good family completely lost and nervous. He was the son of a rich Texan manufacturer, and had never been long from his country or family, that is from his wife and two young children, or his father and mother for that matter. Sometimes he would be in such a slump that after work, a small group of *salarymen* that had taken a liking to him and literally adopted him, would take him *up the ladder* with them, from bar to bar, into the cramped little dives they frequented. Later in the evening, they dragged him along through the little streets of Kabukicho, to clubs where anyone at all could take the mike and bellow out the words to syrupy, soulful songs set to prerecorded music. Every time, the Texan ended up in tears and — to console him — his new friends would then take him to the *pink salons* or *soap-lands*, where he was lavished with care that was at the very least exotic and certainly off-limits even to the imagination. A few times, they ended up in the street too late to take the last metro and the rush for taxis was so great that it was impossible to get one at that hour, even by holding up two fingers to double the price of the ride. The hotel they would end up sleeping in near the train station was like an alveolar cell.

Simon had only spent a few hours in one of these capsular hotels, about six months ago, with a few managers from the firm who absolutely insisted that he experience it. The miniature rooms, which were no more than a metre and a half in height and width and two metres in length, were impeccable, well lit and equipped with a small television. There were several rows of them, piled on top of one another like a chicken coop. Simon found them to have a suspicious resemblance to the refrigerated drawers in the morgues that he had seen in films, and a distant but true similarity to the little compartments where the urns holding the ashes of the deceased are kept. He might have been able to sleep there if he had been completely drunk, but in the only slightly clouded state in which he was floating at three o'clock in the morning, he went into a textbook state of panic and claustrophobia, with almost all the classic symptoms of a coronary. He ended up spending the night in the International Catholic Hospital, where he was kept for six hours, plugged into a high-tech monitor that recorded the slightest quaking of his heart.

Simon had never really had a fit of claustrophobia before but, for the last few years, in certain circumstances he sometimes felt as though a vice grip was clenching his throat to the point where he was very uncomfortable. The first time he'd had that feeling, he was in bed at Chloé's. Since then, the possibility of such a reaction was always waiting there, within him. He didn't know that it could take on immeasurable proportions, though, like the night he thought he was going to die in that little alveolar cell.

The ride to Shinjuku is long because of the traffic, but the large, black taxi is comfortable and air conditioned. The driver is pleasant and very talkative — probably hired because he speaks English uncommonly well — and it is always the same one. Brian had an odd habit of bombarding him with questions about subjects that sometimes seemed to embarrass the man, who nevertheless fulfilled the task of answering politely, though trying to subtly turn the conversation towards other subjects. Simon believes that Suzuki Tatsuo is happy to only have one passenger left — and a silent one at that.

For six months, when the taxi door closes behind Simon, activated by a mechanism on the driver's control panel, he has the impression that the hatch of a bathyscaphe is shutting and locking him in. Though it is cool in the car, Simon fans himself during the entire journey with a folded newspaper that he rocks quickly back and forth with his right hand, like the Japanese do in densely crowded places. The first times Suzuki Tatsuo saw him doing it, he turned the car's air conditioning up right away. But Simon had informed him that it had nothing to do with the heat, so that neither one of them would be cold without reason. By the swift movement, Simon was trying to drive away the anxiety that overtook him as he approached the office where he worked. It was as though, instead of a trip directly across town, from one place in the city to another, the voyage was really a descent into the dark abyss where the taxi would soon leave him to stay, without air, until nightfall. Yet he didn't work underground, below Shinjuku, where people spent their lives working themselves to death, without ever seeing the light of day, in the endless corridors of little workshops, outfits, clinics, stalls, boutiques and department store basements.

Simon works for one of the largest import-export firms in the country, which has to itself the top twelve floors of one of the tallest glass towers in the district. The space on each floor is almost entirely open-concept and you can see out from wherever you are. This doesn't prevent Simon from feeling closed in. Over three hundred people work there at the same time, like in a beehive, visible and on display to everyone, usually in small groups inside an infernal drone.

Kenji, his interpreter, follows him everywhere at work, like a bodyguard. Those were the orders. Where convention and the ways of business were concerned, according to the rank and role of those present, he acted as a secretary and guide for Simon, during business meetings and the evenings out which often came of them.

In the beginning, Simon had asked Kenji several times to leave him alone during the times when he didn't really need him. Each time, Kenji had acquiesced with a bow, repeating *yes, yes, yes*, as though he were about to respect Simon's request, but without stopping his stubborn escort in the slightest. Now, Simon is not at all bothered by the kindly shadow that trails him everywhere.

When the taxi drops Simon off at the front door of the office building, Kenji is already there, as always, though the taxi never arrives at exactly the same time because of unpredictable traffic. But whatever the hour and the weather, Kenji is there outside — with an umbrella if it's raining — waiting for Simon.

Along the way to their offices on the forty-second floor, there is always a manager, here or there, who makes it his duty through Kenji to have a polite conversation with Simon. He is asked about his family, for appearances, without knowing that Simon has been divorced for a long time and that his mother and father are dead. He hears about *sumō* wrestling tournaments and many other things of little interest to Simon. Out of respect, Simon plays along, replying whatever comes to mind, smiling and gently nodding as Kenji translates. These empty exchanges can last forever, as though the person he is speaking to does not dare put an end to the conversation for fear of revealing a lack of courtesy to the foreign consultant. Simon has to wait patiently, like Kenji has taught him, for the other to at last find his way out so that they are free to go their separate ways.

Simon requested that his and Kenji's offices be put near the windows. He also insisted that they be isolated from the crowd by moveable partitions. He was only given one that barely protects him from their line of view, when sitting at a specific angle. It certainly does not prevent the commotion from invading his space. This is where he does his analyses, prepares his files and sends instructions to his office in Montréal for studies and varied field research.

The bulk of his work isn't done in the office, rather throughout the building and elsewhere, often in big conference rooms, where he has to work with engineers, designers, ad executives and a sundry crowd of people who, for the most part, don't speak English. He can work for a company for a few weeks or months, on one or several projects. Then, he is sent to another company which is inevitably affiliated with the huge sprawling firm that hired him.

Though adapting to the new way of functioning was very difficult during the first year, Simon found the novelty and challenge of his work invigorating, a place where he could revel in his insatiable curiosity.

Certain things began progressively to annoy him, irritate him and then completely upset him. Now, he has such a difficult time tolerating them that he wonders how he will manage to see his contract through. Even more so since the meetings have multiplied because he is leaving in eight months.

These collective work meetings have truly become torture sessions. They inevitably begin with the exchange of business cards, then if everyone is not acquainted, they continue with this interminable palaver about the weather, that could sometimes last an hour, as if all these neck-tied, reverent businessmen had simply come for tea. But, the conversation would imperceptibly end up slipping toward the topic of the day and Simon would then be swept into an eddy from which he emerged hours later, often exhausted, empty and nearly ill.

Though all the courtesy-filled and totally idle preliminaries are meant among other things to help Simon integrate — the group having to first ensure its cohesion before being able to work effectively — the part that follows puts Simon into a completely strange position. Despite the fact that he is at the very heart of the meeting, he finds himself entirely exterior to it.

The men, sitting across from him at the other side of the massive table, start a lively discussion in Japanese, which grows increasingly animated as though Simon were not there. Even though he understands basic Japanese, Simon is unable to follow these energetic debates. All the more since they'll soon be talking at once, nearly yelling, shuffling through the piles of documents in front of them, waving a sheet of paper or brochure in the air, displaying on the table or ground minuscule, enormous, sometimes secret objects — packages of noodles, state-of-the-art televisions on the brink of technology and dentists' chairs — drawing sketches, getting out plans, diagrams or tables, projecting and fiddling with synthetic images from sophisticated computers.

You'd think it was a caravansary.

And suddenly, everything stops.

The men turn to Simon and start to ask him, in Japanese, a series of questions that Kenji writes down and translates as quickly as possible on his laptop. The text appears immediately in English on his own screen.

Silence falls sharply on the group.

All eyes rest, riveted, on Simon who first sorts through the questions to indicate which ones require him to do more research or contact his office in Montréal. He starts with the questions that he can answer during the session.

Then he starts to think, rummaging in turn through papers and electronic files, writing down a few ideas. Then he starts to gather his thoughts.

The men in front of him stop moving, they have relaxed into a patience that stands in stark contrast to the feverish display a few moments earlier. This can last for a very long time and it gets harder and harder for Simon to ignore all the scrutinizing eyes while he is thinking and formulating his responses.

When Simon finishes, he signals to Kenji, who begins immediately to translate the answers for the listeners. However, the transfer from English to Japanese takes three times longer than the other way around and, as snatches of Simon's reply come back to them, even when Kenji asks them to wait, the Japanese recommence their discussion and questioning all at once.

After many attempts, Simon and Kenji have developed a relatively fast, effective approach — though it is never fast enough to avoid having his thoughts short-circuited by the continual prerecording of their exchange and new questions that rush forth even before the answers are translated.

What is more, Simon is not speaking his own language. He often uses English for his work but here it is only a relay between French and Japanese, which over time tends to create an imbroglio somewhere inside him, so that sometimes, in the middle of the meeting, he completely loses his bearings.

The results of these meetings always seem to satisfy his business partners of the moment. However Simon, after two years of this routine, is beginning to break down from the inside out.

Nights of insomnia also contribute to a kind of mental paralysis that sometimes comes over him during such work sessions.

Simon knows that Kenji has noticed the changes in him. He says nothing. In fact, outside his function, Kenji speaks very little, so as not to say never. But nothing gets by him.

When Simon feels like he is going to crack, he has come to turn more and more often to Kenji.

CHAPTER 6

The following year, everything changed at the Drouin residence.

In January 1921, Monsieur Drouin started to have a real obsession with the Taschereau government bill proposing to end prohibition and to create a *Commission des liqueurs* to oversee the sale of alcohol in the province.

When the bill was approved in February, the number of visits Monsieur Drouin paid to his brother multiplied. Each time he returned rather drunk and quite flustered indeed. The law was not to come into effect until the first of May and business continued to be good, but Monsieur Drouin was too worried to do anything. Gérard was taking care of everything.

The tension was so great in the house and in the warehouse that Gérard made himself as scarce as possible, not daring to ask the smallest question about what Monsieur Drouin kept calling "their future."

To hear him talk, they were ruined. For awhile, Gérard thought that Monsieur Drouin was talking about himself and his brother. Gradually Gérard came to understand that the situation was not at all catastrophic for Jérôme since he dealt directly with the United States, where prohibition was maintained. When Monsieur Drouin was talking about what was going to happen to them, he was referring to himself, his wife and Gérard, who he called *fiston* — my son. Sometimes, after a long silence, Monsieur Drouin would look up, stick his chin out in Gérard's direction, and say: "What are you going to do, *fiston*? I thought I would be able to leave it all to you some day. Now, it seems like we're finished."

For Madame Drouin, who until then knew nothing about her husband's contraband and imagined that he was earning a living honestly with the vitamins, cough syrup and the water she thought was from Switzerland — the shock was a terrible one. It was even worse when, on the same occasion, she learned that this was far from the first time that he had ever cooked up such a scheme and this had been precisely what had let them lead "such a good life."

The tranquil and serene world in which Madame Drouin had been living crumbled. Everything she had thought simple, fair and good had turned out to be rotten at the core. Without knowing, she had been enjoying the fruit of her husband's dishonesty. She was so ashamed of it all, especially of her own blindness, that she felt unable to talk about it with her confessor and so she stopped going to receive communion.

She forced herself to hide the full amplitude of her reaction from her husband because she had never seen him in such shape. He would not have noticed anything anyway, since he had plunged himself head-first into his own dreadful state.

Gérard, on the other hand, had noticed all the changes in Madame Drouin's behaviour. She didn't wear her fur coat or any of the jewellery her husband had given her anymore. She only wore her house dresses now and never went out except for Sunday Mass. Her eyes were often red and the circles under them had darkened. She had lost her appetite and would stare at the tiny bits of food she put on her plate with obvious disgust.

Gérard was worried about her but he did not dare speak about it because he felt guilty, not simply for having taken part in the trafficking that she so disapproved of, but also for hiding it from her like Monsieur Drouin had. He had also betrayed her confidence in a certain way, that he knew contributed to her grief.

One Sunday evening in February, when Gérard was preparing the cases alone for the next morning's delivery, Madame Drouin left the house without a coat, crossed the garden and burst into the warehouse to "see with her own eyes," she said, attempting to remain impassive.

She walked quickly around the place where she had not set foot for years. A moment later she burst into sobs. Gérard went to console her, but she pushed him away violently. She was crying in rage. Her words cracked, dry and hard. When she left she wasn't crying anymore, Gérard was.

Gérard's feeling of disarray was not because she abhorred his involvement in this affair. In fact, she hadn't openly reproached him about the subject. The most excruciating part for Gérard was to know that Madame Drouin herself felt soiled for being unaware and taking advantage of the "dirty money." It had personally affected her, her own integrity, and that was the part about it that Gérard couldn't stand. He had tried to explain to her that she had nothing to do with it, that she had known nothing about it. But according to her, every mouthful of bread she had eaten and paid for with that money had corrupted her irreparably from the inside.

On May first, when the law came into effect, Monsieur Drouin fell terribly ill. But it was Madame Drouin who died two months later. It happened very quickly and was completely unexpected since all attention had been focused on Monsieur Drouin, who had started to have chest pains.

Madame Drouin had been dragging a bad cold around for months and had grown much thinner. Since the scene in the warehouse, Gérard did not dare speak to her. He watched her waste away from a distance, not venturing a gesture or a word. Monsieur Drouin's health worried him as well. His bouts of chest pain were often spectacular.

Jérôme did not understand how his brother could reach the point of illness over this affair about the *Commission des liqueurs*. He had explained to him clearly on several occasions, in front of Gérard, that he had no reason to worry about his future even if he had to close up shop. Nor would there be a problem if he really wanted to stay in business, said Jérôme. He would simply have to set the price of his *Suisseau Réserve Spécial* below the price set by the *Commission des liqueurs*. According to him, clients who were used to drinking the "real stuff" wouldn't start paying more for something tasteless. They would try it out and quickly return to their good old habits.

At first, his foresight turned out to be right on the mark. But Monsieur Drouin wouldn't give up his idea and was predicting the apocalypse.

Indeed it came, but not in the way he had thought. Madame Drouin's bad cold was in fact a case of tuberculosis that carried her off even before a diagnosis could be clearly established.

Monsieur Drouin's surprise was so great that he forgot at that instant all the anxiety he had about his business and plunged into his own guilt, which was a thousand times worse.

For months, he remained prostrate at home, untouched by everything going on around him, even in the warehouse.

Then one day, Monsieur Drouin asked Gérard to prepare the delivery truck for the next day.

That morning, Gérard watched him leave, dressed in his best suit and felt hat.

When Monsieur Drouin came back that evening, his face had miraculously regained its former appearance, cheerful and teasing. As he came in, he told Gérard that he had been to see "the little women down in the lower town." That very moment, Gérard was overcome with an unspeakable rage that he forced himself to hide.

However, that night, Gérard finally admitted this was probably better than the downtrodden state into which Monsieur Drouin had nearly fallen for good. It was a turn for the better.

The next day at noon Gérard found Monsieur Drouin lying dead in his bed. The day before, on his way to see "his little women," he had gone to the notary and made Gérard his sole heir.

At first glance, the Drouins appeared very comfortable, like most of the people who lived in the neighbourhood, without really being rich. From the outside, their house looked like all the others on the street. However, the inside was furnished and equipped with the best the town had to offer. The carpets were really from Turkey, the porcelain from England and the crystal glassware from Italy.

Monsieur Drouin, like his father and brother, had earned a good trade in a wide variety of fields, which were often a little shady, but had always taken care to hide his slightly dishonest prosperity behind a respectable, unglamorous façade. Even his wife had been taken in. To the point where, when he didn't stop saying for the entire year that they were ruined, she believed it and had imagined that they would really end up in the street, as he had predicted. But rather than upset her, the prospect of it reassured Madame Drouin, as though it would be the best way for her to clear her conscience.

When Gérard was told the actual value of the fortune he was to inherit, he was stupefied. Even if Monsieur Drouin had dropped out of the lucrative traffic in *Suisseau Réserve Spécial*, or any other trade, he and his wife could have lived for two hundred years without worry. Father and son had swindled so much to create all these riches that Monsieur Drouin had never allowed any of it to be displayed. Besides, the seduction of his clientele, in its many forms, had always been much more important to him than the Baccarat crystal chandelier in the dining room and the chic boarding houses they stayed in every summer during their trip to the United States.

Gérard found himself alone in the big empty house, where life could have continued for a long time, sweet and light, if Monsieur Drouin hadn't destroyed it himself.

Monsieur Drouin had let fear creep into their home and devour him and his wife alive. That very fear seemed to have spared Gérard, perhaps because he wasn't really part of the family. But that was merely a front, and Gérard knew it. Fear had not swallowed him up, but it had slipped inside him and sown its seeds — then deserted him.

CHAPTER 7

It is late and Simon dreams only of one thing: going home. Yesterday, after weeks of waiting, he finally received two new pages of "Protective Seals." Maybe more will arrive tonight.

For now, he must stay seated on the floor of the traditional restaurant in Tsukiji, where his bosses have invited him specifically because they are worried about him. They haven't said anything to him, but their concern is revealing.

They have even retained the services of two *geishas* for the evening, at a very high price. They think the women's discreet finesse and the subtle scent of eroticism still fascinate Simon.

For the first two years of his stay here in Japan, Simon observed them as though they were practically insects, trying to understand what these sublimate women are and what is truly at play during these parties, which are at once equivocal and childish, where nothing happens at all. His interest in these women and their exotic, antiquated charms is more that of an entomologist than of a man captivated.

The obsequious attitude of the *geishas* has irritated him from the beginning, along with the nasal sound of their twittering and the meowing of the *shamisen* as the girls scrape the strings with their *bachi*. It's even worse when laughter and other sounds of lute and sitar inevitably fuse with the neighbouring rooms through the fine paper barriers.

The grace and beauty of these women are certainly undeniable, but Simon believes that a much deeper understanding of Japanese culture than his is required to appreciate all the subtlety and power of their ability to fascinate.

Simon can guess at its force, though, by the strange feeling of emotion awakened in him at the sight of their long whitened napes, displayed in the collar of the *kimono* worn low across the shoulders, as they bend down to fill the men's glasses.

This troubling feeling had long surprised him as he remembered the disgust that he felt, during his first trip to Japan, when they told him even before he had met any *geishas* that they once used the excrement of the nightingale to whiten their faces and necks.

Recently, while reading a passage from "Protective Seals," Simon realized that the magnetism of those napes, for him, came perhaps from the repressed memory of another nape, just as graceful and delicate.

Simon knows that he won't be able to remain seated for much longer, smiling and polite, making pleasant conversation, as though nothing were the matter. He is worried that he might jump up and run out screaming, as though the fire had suddenly transformed him into a live torch.

He won't, he knows it, because Kenji is there and he'll help him put an end to this evening before everything turns upside down.

The fact that he has refused practically every invitation for the last few weeks might have been taken for a flagrant lack of civility on his part, the sign of western individualism that is quite petty in the eyes of his hosts. But they've had the time to get to know Simon and they know all the respect he has for them and all the interest that he has for their culture and traditions.

But they do not understand the changes that have taken place in him of late, even physical ones, and they are afraid that he is ill. He agreed to come to this *ryotei* with them to reassure them, and to avoid hurting them. Since the beginning, these men have been infallible with him, facilitating as much as possible his acculturation by creating an easy lifestyle for him in an almost western environment — all the while helping him to gradually take a greater part in the paradoxes of their culture, as he chose.

Simon appreciates the fact that they haven't asked him one direct question about his health or what's going on with him. They seem to trust Kenji entirely to watch over him.

Simon likes the friendliness mixed with reserve that characterizes the men, the distance they constantly maintain with everyone, that they respect in others, all the while attentive and available. He is like them in that way.

Though he is courteous and very sociable, Simon has always kept himself at distance, as though he were hiding in the shadows, secretly observing what is going on around him, curious about what is brewing below even the calmest surface. He was even like that as a youngster. And it was in fact his remarkable capacity for detached, silent observation that allowed him to build a career.

His life, too, incidentally. And that, among others, was what Chloé had reproached him for towards the end. In her eyes, there was nothing admirable about the distance that he maintained between them. Just the opposite. For her, it was like the clear escape route that a fierce animal kept between itself and anything that posed a threat.

Obviously, Simon did not agree with what he called her "diagnostics." She offered them often and with them, the potential to put him beside himself.

He had been the one to suggest that they live together, and Chloé was the one who refused. Just before his departure, he had even asked her to come to Tōkyō with him for three years. He doesn't see how he could have taken his commitment to her any further. Chloé was the one putting distance between them and going against all their plans. He had proof a million times over.

Chloé had burst into his life, the first time, as a veritable apparition on a country road in the middle of the night. Simon was coming back from a friend's cabin party. The rain was coming down in a torrent and the wipers could barely keep the water off the windshield. Suddenly, in the distance, he could make out a woman waving her arms from the side of the road, and he pulled over onto the shoulder. Instead of running towards the car to get out of the rain, she remained motionless before him, caught in the headlights. He got out and, shaking, approached the completely drenched woman, reddened with blood.

People must have been seriously injured somewhere, perhaps caught in the twisted metal of their cars, perhaps killed, their bodies crushed. All this blood on the ground and on the woman could not just have come from her. But Simon wasn't able to turn his head to look around him, on the roadway or in the ditches at the side of the road. His eyes were riveted to the solemn face of this woman, completely unflustered, even strangely calm, as though that night she had gone far beyond herself, once and for all.

He had driven her to the nearest hospital, but had not managed to leave her, even when he learned that her injuries were minor ones. He waited for her for the rest of the night.

In the morning, he took her home to the country — Estrie. The rain had stopped and it was radiantly sunny. She wanted to stop for a moment at the spot where the accident happened.

There were only a few tracks in the grass. Her car had been towed and the stag had disappeared. Chloé had asked Simon what he thought they had done with the animal's corpse. The answer he gave, without thinking, was obvious: "They must have gotten rid of it." The question had taken him by surprise. He never would have thought to ask such a question.

They started driving again. Chloé cried until they arrived.

She made coffee and they drank it on the large veranda at the back of the house, looking out on the river. And without him asking her anything, she told him of another night, eight years earlier, that she had spent alone in the forest, in a similar rain, watching over the bodies of her four-year-old son and her husband, dead in the crumpled Cessna.

She didn't tell him, but Simon was sure that the night before, she held the deer in her arms for a long time before he arrived. Nothing else could explain all the blood on her.

Later they walked in silence along the river.

And, when the time came for him to leave, they made love, without a word, standing near the door of the entry.

CHAPTER 8

At first, Gérard was unable to touch anything in the Drouin's home, though it now belonged to him.

One of Jérôme's sons had called him a thief, going as far as to let there be some doubt about the reason for Monsieur Drouin's death. However, the family had asked for an autopsy and the results clearly showed the cause of death to be myocardial infarctus and that Monsieur Drouin had probably also had two smaller ones in the months before.

In fact, Gérard felt more like a sacrilege than an imposter. The Drouins' whole life was there, spread throughout the house, right down to the most banal objects; Monsieur Drouin's tobacco, left on the pedestal table next to his easy chair, his slippers next to the bed, his glasses on the bedside table.

Madame Drouin's clothes were there too, in the wardrobe. Her ivory and silver hairbrush, comb and mirror set on her dressing table. Her perfume, *Narcisse Noir*, by Caron.

Monsieur Drouin hadn't taken away any of her belongings after she died. Sometimes, when he had drunk a little too much *Suisseau Réserve Spécial*, he opened his wife's sewing basket. He would snip the scissors in the air or try to force the thimble onto his little finger, surprised each time at his wife's delicate hands. Or he would take Blanche's prayer book and look on the sides of the pages for the places that had lost their gold, to try and find the passages she read the most often for comfort, to see if they could help him too. Or he would bury his face in the shawl she left on the back of the rocking chair where she liked to sit. And he would cry.

When Gérard finally dared to advance into their private world, he did it slowly and with a lot of respect. Through all he found in their drawers, the tall cupboards, armoires, in the trunks stored in the attic, the cellar and in the thousand and one metal boxes full of little secrets and souvenirs, their whole history had been given to him without chronological order, as much in the photographs, crocheted tablecloths, letters, bedspreads, dusty hatboxes, as it was in the more emotionally significant items like Madame Drouin's wedding gown, wrapped in blue paper, the pine four-masted ship that Monsieur Drouin had made for his fiancée during their courtship and on the prow of which he had written *Ma belle Blanche*, a wooden horse whose mane had moulded, and a large trunk full of children's clothes and toys.

In the warehouse, Gérard had discovered a multitude of different documents locked in the heavy oak cabinet. Besides all the ones linked to Monsieur Drouin's business — legal and illegal — Gérard found several credit notes by which a few people, who Gérard did not know at all, had promised to reimburse some very high sums of money, with interest, lent to them by Monsieur Drouin.

There was also a veritable collection of photographs of women, dressed scantily in bustiers, basques and tightly laced or stiffened corsets, in garters and black stockings, and on the backs of the photos he found the ruby imprint of a mouth or a desperate love letter and, with them, a pile of little notebooks in which Monsieur Drouin had carefully noted, like a good schoolboy, a few details of each of his adventures, as though he hadn't wanted to forget for a moment, after all the years, the women he had loved.

During the long months Monsieur Drouin had sunk into his bottomless depression, worsened by the death of his wife, Gérard had done everything to keep the business from collapsing, despite the absence of the big boss and the start up of the *Commission des liqueurs*.

Gérard had used every lesson Monsieur Drouin had taught him and, as it turned out, excelled in the art of sales in his own right, even though he didn't have the charisma and roguish charm of his old master. During the "cooking demonstrations," he experienced undeniable success, but the "seduction of the clientele" with him remained on strictly professional ground. And on certain deliveries, when certain individual clients of Monsieur Drouin's made advances, Gérard would launch into an extravagant elegy to his boss, promising the women, who were used to receiving very personal treatment from Monsieur Drouin, that he would be coming back to them in no time at all, friskier than ever, and they wouldn't lose out by waiting for him.

But Monsieur Drouin didn't come back.

And Gérard's business plummeted sharply right after Monsieur Drouin's will was read. Angry that his brother had left his entire fortune, of which a large portion had come from their father's schemes, to a total stranger, Jérôme put an end to all dealings with Gérard, thus refusing him not only the *Suisseau Réserve Spécial*, but also the sulfurous water from Joliette and all its so-called regenerative properties. All Gérard had left were the vitamins and the cough syrup from France.

Jérôme's reaction had been excessive. He liked Gérard, but it was family, "family," and Gérard was not part of it, even though his brother had, in a manner of speaking, adopted him.

In any case, even if Jérôme had reacted differently, Gérard would have found himself in the same situation a few weeks later, and perhaps even worse off when Jérôme and his two sons were arrested for brewing and smuggling alcohol.

In light of the arrests, Gérard thought it best that he go away for awhile, so as not to attract any attention. He also wanted to think about what he was going to do. Besides, he was beginning to turn in circles in the Drouin's home and starting to get a bit down himself.

When he had sorted through Monsieur Drouin's papers, Gérard had discovered a letter that the French company he dealt with had sent him over a year and a half ago. It was to tell him about a whole new line of supplements and natural health products and invited Monsieur Drouin to come and see for himself to eventually, if he chose, open the market in Québec.

When Monsieur Drouin had received the letter, no one had even heard of the bill proposing to end prohibition. Monsieur Drouin was running his golden business with the *Suisseau Réserve Spécial*, and the vitamins and cough syrup only provided the cover. He had let the letter lie on his desk until it was covered by more recent mail.

Gérard contacted the French company and, two months later, he boarded a ship to cross the Atlantic.

It was the first time that he had left Québec, and his several-month stay in Europe was truly his maiden voyage. Even more so because this new world, different yet strangely familiar, was bubbling over after the hard war years.

He returned completely perked up, full of new ideas and projects. It was as though he had managed to detach himself from the past over there and throw himself into the future — his future.

As soon as he was back, he sold the Drouins' house and left straight away for the United States, where, he had been told, interesting research was being done in the field of natural health products.

The two trips had such an effect on Gérard that, when he returned nearly a year later, he was completely transformed, even physically. He had become a man.

In the city, he dressed in full double-breasted suits. He wore a Havana felt hat and chamois gloves. It made him look like a French dandy and American gangster all at once, which seemed to please women enormously.

He moved into a high-class boarding house on Avenue Laval, and devoted himself to starting his business. He rented a small private warehouse that had been neglected near the port and turned it into a laboratory. He hired an apothecary who, from everything Gérard had absorbed in Europe and the United States, started to concoct products with multiple benefits from all natural ingredients.

While his employee was conducting the research, Gérard was travelling the province looking for old wives' remedies and native recipes.

He went out almost every night. The times were roaring and everything seemed light, easy. After a few months, he started to market a few of the products, emphasizing the purity and quality of their ingredients. The "cooking demonstrations" were finished, but had given way to presentations to major potential retailers in medical supplies and pharmaceuticals, religious communities and grocery wholesalers.

Opening these "new market segments" turned out to be very difficult and Gérard suffered many and costly failures. Had it not been for the fortune he had at his disposal and the solid experience he had gained by working with Monsieur Drouin, he would have made quick work of shutting down.

Analyzing the situation, Gérard realized that his products were too austere for the times. So he searched for a way to take advantage of the economic boom following the war and of people's exacerbated need for novelty and exciting new things.

It turned out that it wasn't the products themselves — they stayed exactly the same. It was the vivid, and often exotic, names Gérard gave them and what he started writing on the bottles, boxes and pamphlets that he made available to his potential clientele.

As his employee devoted the time to making these "new" products, often based on very old ways, Gérard started to emit a separate spiel, that was full of promises about his marvellous products and completely in line with the trends of the day. He touted with sparkling style the sublime and even energizing or aphrodisiac powers of the concoctions.

He also changed the slightly harsh containers, which were too similar to those used for medication, replacing them with pretty, decorative flasks and little boxes like the ones used in Europe to sell fine candy.

Things changed in no time at all. While Gérard had originally targeted health and nutrition sectors, the trend and leisure sectors responded massively. Orders for specific products even came in from clubs and dance halls, just as though the products were illegal drugs, likely to increase energy tenfold and allow people to party endlessly without sleeping.

Business was going so well, so quickly that Gérard had to hire a chemist, two people for production and a secretary.

The young woman he hired as a secretary was named Estelle. She was calm and poised compared to all the fleeting creatures Gérard met in the nightclubs he often went to. Her delicate face was opalescent. He was seduced the first instant she came into his office for an interview.

She looked like the *Girl with a Pearl Earring* by Vermeer, which Gérard had seen in a museum in Europe and had stunned him with its astonishing quietude.

Often, when Estelle was working at the typewriter, two steps away from him, he secretly watched the nape of her neck. And the happiness he felt was just how it had been, a few years earlier, when Madame Drouin stood next to him and the sweet fragrance of her narcissus perfume had swept over him.

CHAPTER 9

Simon doesn't agree at all with the timetable that had been set for him with the engineers of a communications firm over the next three weeks. He hasn't finished his last report or sent any numbers back to his office in Montréal as he is supposed to. Even worse, he hasn't had time to fully study the project that he is supposed to work on with the new team. They are imposing busier and busier schedules on him without asking his opinion. He is tired and can't keep up this pace.

He has a cramp in the pit of his stomach. It happens all the time. As though, suddenly, his oesophagus forms a tight knot right above his stomach.

He closes his right fist and presses it discreetly just below his sternum, inside his open jacket. The pain is so strong that it is a real effort not to let anything show.

He also has to stay in control when he explains to Kenji, who must translate for Miki Yoshitaka, the top manager in Simon's section, that the time allotted for the work with this company is much too short, that the meetings need to be further apart to allow him the time to conduct his analyses and write his reports.

Miki Yoshitaka listens to Kenji, smiling and nodding his head, saying *hai, hai!* as though he understands the situation perfectly. But for every answer, he repeats for Simon the programme that had been established without one iota of change.

Simon starts to lose his patience and raises his voice. Kenji calls him back to order with a look.

Instead of getting upset, Simon tries to maintain a state of exterior impasse like the person facing him. He knows by experience that Kenji is right and that an outburst won't get him anywhere and inevitably be to his disfavour. Kenji has taught him how to let the person he's speaking to save face, while still defending his own point of view.

Simon considers his young interpreter, with a diploma from the best university in Tōkyō, the key that allows him to crack the most subtle Japanese codes, and permits him to do his work, avoiding the many quid pro quos and errors committed by most foreign business people in Japan, even after several years.

Simon puts on his nicest smile, uttering a series of *yes, yes, yes!* — like rosary beads meant for Miki Yoshitaka. He then repeats in turn, almost word for word, the request that he has just made, but this time he adds a long roundabout preamble to say that Miki Yoshitaka certainly isn't wrong to think as he does, and that he isn't at all convinced that he knows the right answer, quite the opposite in fact, his opinion is certainly less enlightened than Miki Yoshitaka's, but that another possibility could no doubt still be considered, this, of course, said without wishing to offend Miki Yoshitaka, who is such a wise man...

Simon added a lot. Kenji looks at him and hesitates for a moment, then Simon slips him a smooth yet ironic "Translate, please!" which Kenji ends up obeying. For half an hour, Simon and Miki Yoshitaka play this little game, invariably repeating the same replies, without abandoning for a second the grin that has now formed like a mask at the bottom of their faces.

Tired of the warfare, Simon stands and says in English, with a false modesty that borders on arrogance: *"Am I not at your service, sir? Do as you please! Excuse me, I must leave. Shitsurei itashimasu. Sayonara."* Then he bows to take leave, never abandoning his forced smile, and departs in complete exasperation, before Kenji even has the time to translate. Instead of returning to his office near the windows, Simon heads toward the elevators, ordering Kenji, now running up behind him, not to follow. He leaves the building, hails a taxi and goes to Shinjuku Central Park where he walks quickly despite the humid heat for about thirty minutes, counting his steps as though it were night.

When he returns to the offices, sweating and tired but slightly less tense, Kenji is waiting for him at the main door with a discreet smile on his lips. While Simon was out Miki Yoshitaka had changed his schedule, taking each of his demands into account.

Kenji repeats several times, in a barely audible murmur, as he often does in his sing-song voice: *"Everything will be fine."* It's like a ritornello that spins continuously in this man's head.

It is not the first time — far from it — that Simon has witnessed such a turnaround in a situation that seemed so immutable. He still doesn't understand the mechanisms that are at play during such negotiations where any confrontation must be avoided so that none of the adversaries abandons his viewpoint. In appearance, at least. The turnaround very often only occurs after a long exchange that seems quite sterile, where no one budges. It demands a certain self control that has almost always been within Simon's ability and that his stay in Japan had initially helped to increase. But Simon is losing his grip on himself. Much as he had lost it with Chloé.

Before her, Simon was an unshakeable man, never troubled or moved by anything. Only the birth of his daughter Geneviève momentarily broke open his armour. But after Simon and Sophie's divorce, everything inside had sealed back up and Simon had again become impenetrable, even to Geneviève.

Meeting Chloé had stripped him completely the second their glances met on the small road, in the middle of the night, in the torrential rain. Something had immediately caused a jam in the system Simon had finely tuned since childhood to stay in control of himself and never let anyone — not his father or his wife or anyone — interfere even subtly with his inner self.

During the first months with Chloé, Simon had been carried away by such an astounding and unexpected passion that he had become totally obsessed, without even trying to protect himself.

A little later when reality imposed itself again, the immediate reaction he had was not his usual strategic retreat to avoid a sudden opening and succumbing to this woman's mercy. Just the opposite. He had literally tried to absorb Chloé, to incorporate her into his own existence, to dissolve her inside him, as food is taken into the body.

It was time for him to take his life back into his own hands, with Chloé inside him.

But Simon had met with strong resistance.

Their love had been as unexpected for Chloé as it had for Simon. She had thought she wouldn't ever be capable of loving again after her husband's and son's death, though life had resumed its course with time and flowed smoothly over rough spots.

Before the tradgedy, Chloé lived with her husband and son in Montréal. She was a plastic arts teacher and Jacques was an architect. The week before their Cessna had crashed, they had purchased a house in the country — in Estrie. Something they had long dreamed about. The house was in extreme need of renovation, but it was off the road on a huge lot, bordered on one side by a little river. They had to wait three years for the complex will settlement before being able to acquire the small property.

After the accident, Chloé had plunged into a long depression. For long periods, she left home only for her physiotherapy treatments. With the help of her family, she slowly resurfaced and went back to work.

For three years, she hadn't returned to the house in the country, asking the neighbours to look after it.

One day in May, a real estate agent from the area contacted her to find out whether she was interested in selling it. Chloé hesitated for several days. There was a potential buyer. This had brought back memories that she would have preferred to leave dormant. She made a decision, hoping she could free herself from the pain tied to the property by selling it. She had made an appointment to meet with the agent at the house to discuss certain terms with him and award him with the contract.

She arrived there before him with her sister, in the early afternoon. It had rained a few hours earlier and the sun had just come out. A light mist was rising off the bushes along the river. In the small wood to the left of the house, the young, tender green leaves were translucent and shimmering. In the middle of the slightly wild vegetation, the big house seemed like calm strength.

At that very moment Chloé not only decided to keep the house, but to come and live there permanently.

One year later, after the main floor had been renovated, she did just that. And her healing truly began.

Chloé had been living there for nearly five years when she met Simon.

Simon didn't like the house. Something about it clashed with him, made him a little bit crazy. He would have liked to change it so he could feel comfortable there. But for Chloé this was out of the question.

Their discussions and arguments gravitated around this house, as though everything that caused a problem between them was crystallized in the walls.

CHAPTER 10

Gérard's secretary, Estelle, had grown up in a large family in Richelieu. Her parents were well-known farmers in the valley. She had come to the city with one of her sisters who was going to take a nursing course at the Hôtel-Dieu.

Estelle had decided to take a secretarial course. After receiving her diploma, she returned to live with her parents and worked for two years in a small business in Chambly. But she wanted to go back to the big city and, when she heard through a friend that Gérard was looking for a secretary, she applied.

Estelle was in awe of Gérard from the first time they met. He was only five years older, but his confidence combined with the relaxed elegance he portrayed, both in the way he dressed and the way he spoke, was quite a contrast with the familiarity and bonhomie of her brothers and the men who had courted her until then. She had been so intimidated by Gérard during the interview that she had blushed several times and had trouble answering his questions, even in short sentences. She was convinced that she had acted like a bit of a goose. Yet, after no more than fifteen minutes, she had been hired.

The rest happened just as quickly. Gérard was so afraid of losing this pearl of a woman that they were engaged three months later. The following summer, they were married.

When the time came to send off the wedding invitations, Estelle had written up a long list of friends and relatives that she wanted to invite and asked Gerard to give her his. He replied evasively that he would give it to her soon.

The next night, he didn't sleep a wink. He didn't have a single name to put on his list. Of course he had business relations and his friends from the bars, he was also very close with several women, whom it would have been very improper to invite to the wedding. Real friends and relatives, he had none. He had severed all ties with his aunts, uncles and cousins, and he didn't even know if his father was still alive. The only people he would have wanted to be at the reception were the Drouins. Gérard contemplated the extent of his solitude and it shook him.

He informed Estelle the next day that, apart from one of his employees, who would stand up for him, he didn't have any guests. When she expressed her surprise, Gérard refused to discuss it.

Despite the blatant imbalance on the day of the wedding, Gérard completely forgot that he was the only one on his side. Not because he had entered into a big clan that had welcomed him warmly, but because a few hours later when the celebration had ended, he knew he would be leaving with Estelle, his wife. And that's all that mattered to him.

Gérard took Estelle to Paris for their honeymoon. He wanted to "give" her the city, whose charms he had succumbed to several years earlier.

On their return, they moved into a huge Victorian house on Saint-Denis, which Gérard had purchased shortly after their engagement.

Gérard truly worshipped his wife. His affection for her was boundless. For him, she was all women united, the Whole, the Only, the One, the woman in whom all others, even the mother he had never known, were included — incorporate.

Starting a family was of little importance to Gérard. Estelle was now his wife and that would have been enough for eternity. Estelle, on the other hand, wanted many children. Granting her this pleasure was not a problem at all for Gérard. He couldn't very well ask her to stay at home all alone, with nothing to occupy her day, like Madame Drouin, while he was at work.

They were blessed the first time with a baby boy. At birth, Claude was puny and sickly but under the good care of his mother and grandmother, he gained strength quickly.

In Gérard's mind, Claude was not so much his son as a gift he had given to his true love. While pregnant, Estelle had been radiant and becoming a mother made her even more beautiful.

Less than a year later, she was pregnant again. Marie arrived amid the summer heat. She was a whiny baby, in need of constant reassurance and rocking. She had her mother's grey eyes, but she was so pale it seemed as though she didn't have any blood.

The huge house gradually came alive. All of its life was organized and gravitated around Estelle — she was its centre, its heart.

The children left Gérard completely indifferent. In fact, he saw very little of them. But for his wife, he had all the attention in the world, returning with a small surprise for her almost every night. He often came home late, since the business was in full growth, but Estelle would wait to have dinner with him, sometimes until nine o'clock.

Then the Crash of 1929 and the dark years of the Depression descended on them.

Financially, Gérard was less affected by the economic crisis than most people, but he had to completely redesign his products.

The times were no longer booming. Hundreds of unemployed lined up outside the city shelters and soup kitchens. It was out of the question for people to be buying sexual stimulants or little pills with explosive effects for amusement. It was first necessary to find enough to eat, which was not easy. There was no more work and entire families, who had always thought themselves safe from poverty, ended up in complete misery.

In spite of radically plummeting sales, Gérard decided not to lay off his employees, but he had to substantially reduce their salaries.

Although Gérard knew that he wasn't talking about some cheap universal remedy, he'd had to knit quite a hazy discourse around his products to be able to sell them during the roaring twenties, in keeping with the times of the day. His travels in Europe and the United States, and the research he'd done in Québec all aimed to create a line of natural medicinally based products, mostly based on very old recipes. For different reasons, his products didn't qualify as official pharmacopoeia, but that didn't mean their properties were not real.

Gérard decided to make the remedies readily available to all, with a view to keep his company afloat. From the line of products he chose those richest in vitamins, minerals and trace elements, putting the less appropriate ones aside for awhile. He came back to the standard containers and found a comforting name and description for each product to evoke an image of hope during the years of complete slump. The words "nutritional supplement" were repeated constantly. When people couldn't feed their children, they could at least give them a few supplements so they weren't completely debilitated by the depression.

For two years, Gérard renounced all personal benefits, selling at wholesale prices and often agreeing to give credit when it was obvious that he would never be fully reimbursed. He even gave hundreds of cases away to the religious communities, who would distribute the "nutritional supplements" to those who needed them most, with special mention of where they had come from.

Gérard's generosity gave Estelle boundless admiration for her husband.

With Gérard's permission, she did her part by converting the empty rooms in their house into a temporary refuge for mothers who found themselves literally in the street with their children. The government's *Secours direct* often wasn't enough and wasn't available to everyone.

During this time, another daughter, Dominique came into the family. She was a strong child who almost never cried and laughed constantly, like her mother, who she resembled.

Despite the morose atmosphere that still loomed everywhere, their home remained happy and lively. In good conscience, Gérard and Estelle were able to enjoy in peace the happiness they would have found indecent had they not somehow helped their fellow citizens get through the hard times.

Slowly, after many difficult years, social change finally took effect and things started to improve. Life gradually found a normal rhythm again.

Gérard's business improved as a result. The reputation of his products was now solidly established. He gradually raised the prices, but only to set them at a completely reasonable level so that they could slowly become a household necessity, like bread and milk. With certain vitamins, he even gave away a container with compartments in the same pattern as the dishes of the day to put on the table with the sugar bowl, the salt and pepper shakers, so that every morning children developed the habit of taking their daily vitamins.

Gérard now emphasized the fact that his products were based on the oldest of recipes. He couldn't explain why, but he felt that people needed, at the end of the Depression, to return to the remedies of their ancestors to heal their hearts and give them strength.

In early 1937, Estelle was pregnant again. The news made her very happy, since she loved the house to be brimming with life.

Gérard, for his part, loved it when his wife was happy.

The pregnancy was easy, like the first three, except that two weeks before the delivery date, Estelle's blood pressure dropped causing her to suffer from dizzy spells.

One morning, as she was about to walk down the stairs, she felt dizzy and fell.

As she tumbled, she hurt her forehead and fractured her ankle. Her water broke and her contractions started suddenly, painfully.

Though the cut near her temple wasn't serious, Estelle's face was covered in blood. Gérard, who had come running when he heard her cries and had seen her crumpled at the bottom of the stairway, was seized by panic. He wailed his wife's name, his head in his hands, unable to do a thing to help her. The children were howling too, in tears around him.

Estelle was the one who eventually took charge. Trying to calm Gérard, she asked Claude, who was ten, to go ask the woman next door for help.

She gave birth on the floor at the bottom of the stairs, while Gérard sat in the living room, shattered.

The mother recovered in no time. But the father never recovered. One of the seeds of fear inside him had begun to take root.

For Estelle, the fact that the baby was safe and sound was a miracle. She named the little girl Denise and took care of her jealously, as though to free herself from her guilt of not giving her the gentle birth she had given the others.

Gérard never managed to love the child. He tried to ignore her, even more than the others, though she was the most like him in every way. It was uncanny.

CHAPTER 11

When he arrived in Japan, Simon was not sure he liked the fact that his company had rented a studio for him in a completely Western apartment building. He would have much preferred the feeling of strangeness, to go live in the most traditional villages of Tōkyō, like Nicholas, a Frenchman to whom he had been introduced a few months after his arrival. He teaches in a university and has lived in Kagurazaka for eighteen years with his family, and he has integrated perfectly with neighbourhood life.

But now Simon appreciates the choice made by his hosts. Everything has become so unstable inside him that he needs this calm and familiar place. The decor in his studio is elegant and refined, without a bit of clutter. And a housekeeping service sees to everything, just like in a hotel.

His studio is now the only place where Simon feels slightly sheltered from the megalopolis that he has perceived for some time now as a gigantic octopus that is trying to touch him, stick to him and wind its many tentacles around him.

Simon had originally explored the city from a distance — with the art of maintaining space not only between himself and whatever threatens him, but also between himself and whatever fascinates him — in such a way that he can venture into any landscape with complete impunity and discover its most secret, intimate recesses without ever really being affected by them.

This distance has melted away progressively without his realizing or knowing how such a transformation could have occurred inside him. Now he is at the mercy of the world into which he thought he was gradually foraying, conquering. The paradoxes are cracking his armour.

Simon can no longer see the hidden coherence of this disparate universe into which he has chanced without protection. He has the impression that millions of small-scale thoughts, ways of being and doing have been glued together any which way to form this colossal monster, without head or tail or anything recognizable, where all truths explode from endlessly penetrating and contradicting one another.

Even the architecture of the city, where Simon once perceived a creative, baroque burgeoning, now attacks and upsets him. It's all a hotchpotch of fashions, styles, and eras, detached from their historical or cultural references, uprooted and stuck next to one another, with nothing holding them together except the omniscient noise — like glue.

Simon likes things that are clear and defined, univocal. Those that are not have always seemed exterior to him. He considers any irresistible attraction he feels to be simple, scientific curiosity.

But this reasoning no longer holds sway. Now everything, including himself, is discordant. Something has come loose, and he can't seem to stick the pieces back together.

Chloé's house provoked this same explosion in Simon. That is why he initially preferred to stay only occasionally and then, afterwards, his visits became rarer and rarer.

For months, Chloé was the one to go to his place, the big apartment overlooking the river.

Then, out of spite, she decided to go to Simon's only if he came to her place too.

They ended up seeing each other in hotel rooms.

At Simon's, everything was expensive, though plain and in perfect taste. Chloé said it was completely antiseptic. According to her, no germs could grow there, nor could it sustain any other life form.

At Chloé's there were zones. Some completely light and others perfectly sombre and deleterious. Simon said that it was a charming place, but needed to be redone. He even talked about tearing the whole house down to build another one — their country house — at his cost. Chloé ended up coming to live with him, in his spacious apartment. He rented her a studio in the same building for a workshop.

Even the main floor, which Chloé had completely redone, got on
Simon's nerves. Mostly because it had the misfortune of being located
between the basement and the second floor. Simon could not get away
from the idea that above his head, there was an entire world that was
dark and suffocating, while below his feet, the space was cluttered in
an unfathomable jumble where things had started to mould and disin-
tegrate in the moisture of the bare earth.

What also surprised Simon about the main floor was that Chloé
had renovated it in a completely anarchist way. It had undeniable
appeal, but nothing met the ordinary criteria used to design a living
space. Nothing was in its place. There was no living room, kitchen or
dining room. Everything was everywhere, spread out according to
Chloé's whim. Simon could not comprehend the logic that governed
her kind of organization.

The first thing you saw upon entry was a large space that looked
out on the river, with an entire wall of windows and glass doors. There
were also many openings in the adjacent walls. Light seemed to be
Chloé's priority, probably because she was a painter.

Only the façade still had all its tiny windows, a reproduction of the
original model. Simon didn't understand Chloé's choice that had split
the style of the house so that it was hybrid, poorly designed and ugly.
Furthermore, in the part looking out to the front, Chloé had hung little
lace curtains in the windows and carelessly put around a few old pieces
of furniture. Among others, there was a small, straight chair that was
turned stubbornly to face the wall. Each time Simon arrived, he turned
it around. While he was there, the chair stayed like that, but as soon as
he left, it was returned to its unusual position facing the wall.

The rest of the massive room was Chloé's workshop and living
space in one. It was in perpetual disorder, which was nothing unpleasant for Simon, though it matched nothing in his world. He took
pleasure observing this sort of fantasy world that fit his image of
Chloé perfectly.

In his eyes, the rest of the house was simply there, around him, by
accident, as though Chloé had just not gone to the trouble or found the

means to make its strange appendages disappear; he thought he could easily take care of this.

It was nevertheless on the main floor where Simon felt the least threatened — when he managed to forget what was above and below him.

Chloé's bedroom was on the second floor. Simon had always refused to sleep there, not out of stubbornness, but because he couldn't handle it.

Contrary to what Simon believed, Chloé had the money to renovate the upstairs of the house. Yet, only a few absolutely necessary changes had been made. Chloé had preferred to give herself the time, at her own pace, to domesticate this house that was so loaded with history.

The second floor was sombre, slightly like a maze with narrow hallways, nooks and tiny little rooms that were so small you couldn't even guess what they had once been used for. You would have thought they were storage spaces. But there were so many that, apart from the two slightly larger bedrooms and the cramped bathroom, they took up the whole space. With their sloping ceilings, some of them were impossible to enter without hunching over. Some didn't have windows and in the ones that did, the windows didn't open because successive coats of paint had sealed them up. Both panes were dirty and many insects had died between them. In some of the tiny rooms, Chloé had stored her painted canvases.

The paintings were on the floor, leaning side by side against the boards of the old walls. When Simon had discovered this strange gallery, he had been bowled over as much by the power of Chloé's pieces as by the fact that she left them like that, hidden in this condition.

They had violent arguments about her work. Simon spoke of the waste. He wanted Chloé to meet one of his friends, owner of a well-known gallery on Rue Sherbrooke, and have an exhibit. She refused to hear any of it. One day, without telling her, Simon arrived at her place with his friend to show Chloé's paintings and strange sculptures, in the woods near the house. As soon as she understood that it was the gallery owner, she had kicked Simon out, along with his friend.

In Chloé's bedroom, the windows were new. They were the same model as the old ones, double panes that opened wide. The wooden walls and ceiling had been painted white, like the floor. In fact, absolutely everything in her room was white and it was almost empty, except for the big iron bed, night table and reading lamp. The walls were bare and there were no curtains.

The other room had been partially fixed up, like Chloé's. It was white, but completely empty. Simon had asked Chloé what she planned on doing with it. She had answered: "Nothing." Simon had wanted to hang some of Chloé's work and put in appropriate lighting, until she decided to "do something with her work." But she refused.

Above the second floor, there was an attic pierced with six small dormer windows. Because of the slope of the roof, their height was reduced. Simon had gone up with Chloé one summer day. The heat was suffocating. But Simon absolutely insisted on seeing what was up there. Chloé had left everything there when she and Jacques had bought the house. Cluttered *pêle-mêle*, the objects left by the former owners had been stored there over the years — the things they no longer used but were unable to throw or give away. A large silvering mirror, now completely destroyed, trunks full of moth-eaten clothing, piles of books with stiff, yellowed pages and an old rattan *landau* with caved-in weaving. The entire floor was covered, as were the sloping walls where hats, skates, parts of a harness and a thousand other things had been hung on nails. Chloé hadn't touched a thing. It was all covered in dust.

Simon had suggested that they sort through the *bric-à-brac* which contained certain valuable items that they could keep, including a very old, unsigned painting, that he would have wanted to have identified and appraised, and other objects for which they could barely guess their use. He at least wanted to get rid of what he thought made the attic insalubrious, particularly an old armchair that the mice had claimed as home. She refused. Once the trap door had closed, they never went up to the attic again.

To Simon, the basement was more upsetting than all the other parts of the house. Chloé had heaped up most of what had belonged to her son and her husband, right on the bare earth.

If she had taken care to preserve all these things from the humidity and the rodents, perhaps Simon could have understood that she hadn't yet managed to part with them, but he found it totally inconceivable that she let it all rot slowly under her feet, rather than get rid of it altogether.

CHAPTER 12

From that point on, nothing was ever the same. Gérard now called his wife several times a day, worried about her for any little reason, jealous of the children, to whom she devoted almost all of her time and who, according to him, were exhausting her.

After Denise was born, Gérard had declared that this was the end of the family. Estelle didn't agree — she was only thirty-two — but Gérard had changed so much and he was so anxious that she didn't dare to argue with him. He had actually taken the responsibility of calculating the time of her ovulation and writing it on a calendar, to avoid "the worst," as he put it.

When Gérard was at home now, the ambience solidified around him. Everything turned icy, though he never raised his voice. The children preferred to seek refuge in their rooms or in the playroom, or to go to the park or to their friends' homes.

Except Denise, who was too small to be away from her mother and who nevertheless tried to go to the man who pushed her away coldly each time, as you would push away a dog under foot.

With Estelle, Gérard was still as considerate and attentive, but his loving concern now bore the mark of such worry that Estelle suffocated beneath it.

When her mother came to spend a few days at their house, Estelle took advantage of the time to get out and do volunteer work. Leaving the house did her the most good.

The war had started to spread through Europe and, though the Canadian government had not yet imposed general conscription, the whole population was asked to get involved in the war effort.

Gérard didn't like it when his wife spent time away from the house. This was the subject of their first arguments. Gérard agreed to Estelle's volunteering, but from home. Several women made their contribution in this way. That wasn't what Estelle wanted. He knew that, and it irritated him. He gave the pretext that a good mother should stay at home to take care of her children. But she held out against him for the first time in her life.

Later, they had greater conflict on another subject. On July 14, 1940, the German army had marched into Paris. Since Germany had invaded Belgium and Holland, Gérard was in favour of making military service compulsory for single men and widowers without children, and overseas service as well. Until then, only volunteers enrolled and went over to fight with the Allied troops on the Old Continent. These issues were already the subject of flaming debates throughout Québec and Canada.

On July 4, Gérard came to blows with his wife's two youngest brothers in Richelieu. Encouraged by their whole family, including Estelle, they had decided to get married on the same day to women with whom they were obviously not in love. Just to escape recruitment. According to the law making military service mandatory for all single men, passed on June 18, all the men who weren't married before July 15 would have to enlist.

Paris was occupied and those "young hicks" were only worried about "finding a hideaway" so they wouldn't have to go fight for the mother country. They were even talking about getting their wives pregnant as soon as possible in case the call extended in future months to include married men without children. Gérard was beside himself.

When they started back, right after the clash, everyone in the car was silent for the whole trip home. As soon as they reached the house, the children disappeared into their rooms, and Estelle and Gérard fought.

From that day on, Gérard never returned to Richelieu for anything other than funerals. He agreed to letting Estelle's mother come and stay for awhile with her daughter, but they no longer went to family celebrations, even Christmas.

Estelle experienced enormous grief. But in spite of appearances, the loss was even greater for Gérard.

By cutting off ties with Estelle's family, he really was alone. Estelle was no longer with him, she sided with her family. Gérard had gone too far, he had said things to his wife that he regretted, but couldn't undo any of it.

For the summers that followed, Estelle would leave with the children to spend several days with her family in Richelieu.

From the first time Estelle was gone, Gérard fell prey to insidious jealousy. Deep down, he knew that his wife was faithful to him. Yet, when night fell, his doubts seized his spirit and tormented him. To stop the whirlwind in his head, Gérard would go out. His heart wasn't in it, however, and all his mean adventures only left him with a bitter taste in his mouth. He did not like the man he had become.

When Estelle came back, he tried again to be the lover he had been before this madness had seized him. He did everything to be forgiven. But even after Estelle had forgiven him, he couldn't manage to attach himself to her as he once had.

Then, completely unexpectedly and despite all Gérard's precautions, "the worst" happened. Ten years after her fall down the main stairway, Estelle was pregnant again.

When he learned the news, Gérard iced over and left for work without a word.

Upon his return, very late that night, he told Estelle that there was no way she was keeping this child. She was forty-one and she had nearly died during the last delivery. That day, he had spoken to a friend who was a doctor, who had agreed to perform a therapeutic abortion the next morning in his clinic.

Stupefied, Estelle refused.

Her opposition sent Gérard into such a rage that Estelle thought he was going to strike her. He had never acted like this.

Things ended with him screaming, for no good reason, that this child couldn't be his and walking out, slamming the door.

All night, Estelle cried.

Part Two

"If you want the nut,
you have to crack the shell."

— Maître Eckhart

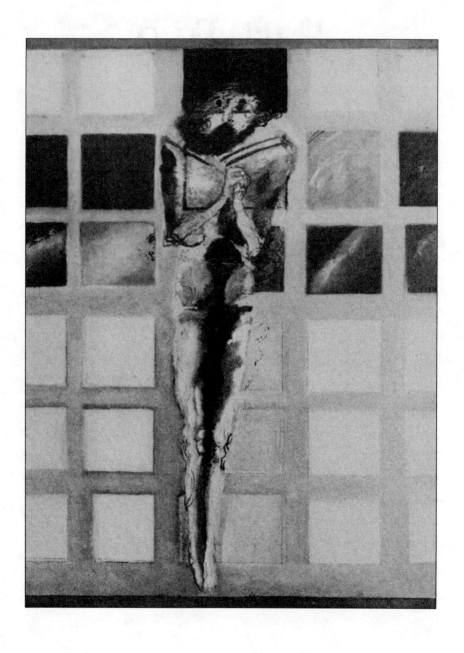

CHAPTER 13

Simon could very well be in California, the decor of this extremely trendy restaurant in Roppongi is so identical to the one in Los Angeles by the same name, where he has been twice. A few of the Americans he knows from here, two of whom are going back to the United States tomorrow, only come to this type of place, certain there is no risk of feeling displaced. Simon has despised this attitude for a long time. Now he envies the psychological stability that they have been able to preserve and go home with, while he breaks apart a little more each day.

For the last six months, Simon hasn't joined in on any of these evenings — just tonight — Sue, an American he was with for almost a year, is one of the ones leaving.

Very soon after his arrival, the small community of consultants and North American students working in Tōkyō welcomed Simon. It was part of the tradition, as was celebrating departures.

Simon took a while to become a part of the group. After long days of adapting to a completely new way of working, he had to respond to invitations from the people in the firm that employed him. They went out every night. As though the men in this company never went home, except on Sunday.

When Simon finally returned to his studio, he would continue his never-ending discussions with Chloé over the Internet.

It was only once their bond began to weaken that Simon began to accept the invitations from the small group of North Americans.

Until then, despite the distance separating them, Simon never felt far away from Chloé. They had found a meeting place, somewhere above the ocean, in a strange dimension that was somehow very real for him.

Now that they had nothing left to say to one another, Simon felt truly alone without really suffering. He had felt exactly the same when his mother died and after his divorce.

He didn't miss Chloé. In fact, he felt nothing, as though his innards had been taken out and he had been stuffed. At night when he was lying on his bed, sleepless and motionless, he concentrated on following the movement of his breathing and feeling the heartbeat in his chest. For Simon, this was a clear sign that he was not actually dead.

Sue had also been such confirmation.

He watches her laugh from the other side of the table. The way she let her head fall back when she laughed had been the first thing that had made him desire her. As though everything with this woman could be light, airy, without consequence. "Normal," Simon had thought.

For him, relationships had to be this way. When things became complicated with his ex-wife, Sophie, he had left. And when he had understood that nothing could be simple with Chloé, he accepted the the Japanese firm's offer.

Sue is more like Simon than Chloé. She's a determined woman, who manages her life exactly the way she manages her work. She possesses a surprising alloy of tension and nonchalance that gives a woman an almost brutal charm, even physically. She learned her business from her father who, without the son he had hoped for, had instead taught his bright, curious daughter everything he knew. From the age of twelve, as soon as she was on holidays, she insisted on going with him to the furniture factory. She was willing to do anything, even sweep the floors, to be there with her father, in the place where she breathed the sweetest scents in the world — wood, glue and varnish. Gradually her father let her into his universe. For her twenty-first birthday he gave her shares in the company, and officially added *and girl* to its name. When her father died, Sue inherited the company. She was only twenty-six then. She had to fight against a group of small stockholders who held the most important positions in the company and did everything to get her to allow them to run the business on her behalf. She held her ground and two of them ended up quitting.

Sue would have liked to spend her last night in Tōkyō with Simon. She asked him awhile ago. He replied that he couldn't, with no explanation. She wouldn't ask for one, just as she didn't insist when she was recently worried about him and he told her that everything was really fine, even though he definitely looked unwell.

Simon put an end to their affair when he started to receive bits of "Protective Seals." He was soon to make an appearance in the story. Perhaps even tonight. For now, he is inside Estelle's belly. He is "the worst," that his father so feared and wanted to avoid. Simon doesn't doubt this any longer.

When he broke things off between them, Simon didn't explain anything to Sue. In his eyes, it was unnecessary. She knows nothing about him, as he knows nothing about the life she is going back to in two days, her home in Oregon. Perhaps she has a husband or children? Sue knows about Geneviève, Simon's daughter, only because she came to spend the Christmas season in Tōkyō. Otherwise, he would never have mentioned her.

Chloé did not understand this attitude. It was by accident that she had discovered, nearly a year after meeting Simon, that he had a daughter.

Simon had gone shopping when Geneviève rang at his apartment and asked Chloé over the intercom to open the door so she could see her father. She had just argued with her mother.

At first, Chloé thought it was a mistake.

When Geneviève came into the apartment, she looked Chloé up and down and hurled out at her, "So Dad likes them old these days!"

She threw her enormous carry-all on the floor, pulled off her platform shoes and threw them into the middle of the room, then tumbled onto the living room sofa.

Chloé stood in the doorway for a minute, flabbergasted.

Geneviève had the dishevelled head of a sea bird. Her hair, electric blue, was bristled and formed a sort of crest on top. Her eyes had so much makeup on them that she looked as though she was wearing a dark velvet eye mask. Her body was thin and her legs seemed so long in her tight leather pants that she looked like a wader bird.

Simon took a while to get back and it was more than difficult for Chloé to make conversation with the tall, escaped adolescent. Chloé's attempts at friendliness were of no use. Geneviève showed open hostility toward her. After an hour, Chloé took her things and left.

Later, Simon phoned Chloé and, furious, she reproached him for never mentioning that he had a daughter. And he answered that he had simply not seen the necessity since it didn't concern her. She started screaming at the other end of the line. Simon was always taken aback by this sort of reaction in Chloé. He ended up losing control as well.

Simon was a compartmented man. Certain aspects of his existence were walled in behind barriers so firm that Chloé sometimes had the impression he came out of nowhere, that he was always what he is now, the product of a spontaneous generation, without a childhood or parents like everyone else, without a past. She didn't even know exactly how many brothers and sisters he had, and she had never met any of his family. When she questioned him on the subject, his responses were always evasive and laconic, and she never managed to get anything out of him. If she insisted, he grew cross, as though she were trying to pull secret information out of him so she could use it against him later.

Chloé ended up regretting telling him everything about herself, spontaneously, during their days together, and introducing him to her family and friends, when the truth was that she knew nothing about him. When she reproached him for it, he told her that he was not hiding anything from her, that there was frankly nothing interesting to know. He loved her and wanted to live with her, that's what was important to him. But it wasn't enough for Chloé.

At those times, Simon found Chloé not only complicated, but unpredictable. She could be calm and lucid for days but then everything would change in one motion, at the slightest thing. Without Simon's even expecting it. The most insignificant word, the most banal subject could suddenly release the storm within her, which then took an eternity to calm.

That's what had happened when she discovered Geneviève's existence. She had brought it up for months afterwards, not only trying to find out more about his daughter and Simon and Sophie's life together, but also to understand his obstinate silence about everything that was him.

He couldn't see the point in rehashing all those past events.

What upset Simon was that, with Chloé things never ended up being simply what they were. She always seemed hooked into a network of underground tunnels where everything was obscurely entangled in a tightly wound skein of repressed memories, images and impressions.

CHAPTER 14

Like Denise, Simon had his father's amber eyes and looked unmistakably like him.

Despite the totally misplaced jealousy that had nearly made him sick during Estelle's pregnancy, Gérard soon gave in to the evidence — Simon was definitely his son. This changed nothing about his feelings toward him.

All these children had ended up robbing him of his wife, and the last one was going to push his outrage beyond a point he could manage.

The day after the stormy evening that Gérard asked Estelle to have an abortion, when he finally came home in shambles the next morning, he shaved, took a long shower, got dressed, ate breakfast, kissed his wife, and went off to work. Just as though nothing had happened.

Then events took their course, with no more discussion about the scene.

During Estelle's entire pregnancy, Gérard was considerate to her, faultlessly so, just as he had been in the past. But this time, it was not really out of love or caring. He was simply doing what he thought he should, to the best of his ability, haunted each day by the possibility that everything would suddenly explode inside him and push him to do something irreparable.

All his energy was consumed by contradictory and insane thoughts that overtook him and tore him apart night and day. He could swing from one extreme to the other, without a word, at one instant wanting to kill Estelle and the next ready to give his life so that nothing would happen to her.

When his mind was clinging to the idea that his wife had cheated on him, Gérard imagined for hours on end demented scenarios where masses of isolated details fit together perfectly like a puzzle and which took on a sense that had nothing to do with reality. Once they were pieced together, they seemed to form such a cohesive whole that Gérard allowed himself to be totally convinced, incessantly finding new elements to support his wildest suppositions.

He even reached the point of imagining that his wife was pregnant by the parish priest. Estelle had done a lot of volunteer work in the church basement, the priest was her confessor and she went to see him a lot more often than she used to. These suspicions got to the point that Gérard stopped going to Mass because he was unwilling to take any risks.

But the scenario that Gérard harboured most, and returned to most often, was the one where Estelle's brothers, out of pure vengeance, introduced her to a man who became her lover. The dates more or less matched those of Estelle's last visit to Richelieu.

When he managed to calm his jealousy for awhile, Gérard feared that Estelle would die in labour. She even had the same fainting spells as she had during her last pregnancy. She was tired and less radiant than the other times. She almost never laughed anymore.

Gérard had put a bed in the living room so that she didn't have to go up and down the stairs and didn't risk falling like she did with Denise. Estelle had protested, but to no avail. When he was there, she respected his instructions, but as soon as he left she did what she pleased.

Taking advantage of a moment when Estelle was out of the house, Gérard held a family meeting with the children. He painted such a fearsome portrait of their mother's supposedly difficult pregnancy that they all, with the exception of Denise, felt guilty without really knowing why. They had a distant but absolutely upsetting memory of Estelle's fall down the stairs ten years before. While her brother and sisters bowed their heads in shame listening to their father, Denise stared defiantly at Gérard throughout his entire pompous and alarmist speech.

Their eldest was now twenty. Over time, Gérard had succeeded in making Claude a failure. He had started early, as soon as he had felt that his son could be a rival to him, that is when he was still just a baby.

During his childhood, Claude had been protected by his mother. He was asthmatic and had such spasmodic croup attacks that his mother thought he would never recover.

During his adolescent years, everything turned around. Though he had always been small for his age, he started to grow and develop all at once. In a few months, he caught up with the tallest in his class. But his father continued to think of him as a low-calibre weakling. He made Claude work at the business during his days off and vacations. Gérard merely assigned him subordinate tasks, constantly supervising him and taking note of the smallest errors. At home, when there were more difficult jobs to be done and Claude offered to help his father, he would wave him off without one look, saying, "No, no. Go and rest. You'll tire yourself out."

Marie, on the other hand, was a pale, daydreamy young woman of eighteen, who seemed to be permanently elsewhere. She read romance novels and waited for her Prince Charming. She was not at all bothered by the fact that Gérard never paid her any attention. For a long time, it fascinated her to quietly observe Estelle and Gérard. She often asked her mother about how they had met, the gifts he had given her, the honeymoon they had taken. She would have liked to know everything — the sweet words he had for her, his tender touch. She watched the loving looks Gérard poured over her mother. At one time they'd had the power to make Estelle bloom, even when she was tired. Marie's greatest dream was to one day meet a man who would love her like her father loved her mother. Yet, the only men she attracted were those seeking a little adventure, to whom she gave herself fully, and who left her just as soon with a broken heart. Though Marie had Estelle's milky skin and grey eyes, Gérard didn't like the insipid, silly gaze that she often trailed across him.

Fifteen-year-old Dominique was such a healthy, lively girl she gave off the impression that her father's coldness didn't affect her. Perhaps, she thought confusedly, that he wasn't completely unaware of her. Sometimes Gérard watched his daughter, without her knowing, and had to stop himself from going to her, taking her in his arms, the resemblance to her mother when they had first met was so great.

Though she was only ten years old, Denise was the rebel in the family. After having sought her father's affection for years and crying many times alone in her room because he had pushed her away, she did an about face.

One summer, Gérard had decided that when school was finished Denise would return for six weeks to Portland, Maine, for summer camp. Though she had hated the experience the summer before. She died of loneliness, even more so since visits were forbidden — so the children wouldn't be upset — and since her birthday happened to be during the stay. Besides, when Denise arrived at the camp, she didn't speak a word of English. Gérard said that immersion was precisely how to learn a new language, just as he had done, and that she would thank him for it later.

Denise had cried, begging Gérard not to send her back there, saying she wanted to stay with them for her vacation. Gérard retorted that it was precisely because she was always around that Estelle was tired and needed to rest.

One afternoon, when he saw that Denise wasn't giving up and kept coming back to the subject, Gérard ended up swinging a sledgehammer of an argument at her, which he believed would quieten her once and for all. He grasped her by the arms and said to her in a low voice, from behind clenched teeth a few centimetres from her face, "You already nearly killed your mother once. I won't let it happen again!"

His strategy didn't have quite the effect he hoped.

Denise moved away slowly. She looked her father in the eye and, after a brief silence, she said to him, strangely calm, "You're mean because you're afraid."

Then she left with no particular rush, without leaving his gaze until she had gone through the door.

Gérard remained motionless for a moment, shaken. Denise's words and distant attitude, along with the penetrating gaze she let rest upon him for the first time, revealed that despite her young years she had known for a long time something extremely painful and secret about him, something that he would have never believed she could see.

That day, even though Denise had never been a difficult child, Gérard decided that he was going to break her.

CHAPTER 15

The decibel level is record high today, feverishness and euphoria reign throughout Simon's office building, the streets and the entire city.

Simon is so overwhelmed by the agitation and by the laughter that goes off endlessly around him that he hasn't done any work since this morning. He has put in *Quies* ear plugs, and from the window he is watching this great city that everyone is getting ready to desert.

Kenji, at his desk, does not seem bothered in the least by the frenzied environment that surrounds them. For hours now, he's been concentrating on finishing the translation of a report that Simon gave him at the beginning of the week.

The effervescent business district known as Shinjuku, like Manurouchi, will soon empty for a few days and appear nearly dead.

Since he started so late, Simon has been unable to find an airplane or even a train ticket to get to Kōya, the only place he feels like going at the moment. During the short vacation, everyone leaves at once and everything is booked everywhere, far in advance.

Simon would like to go back to the great Kōya-san Buddhist monastery, nestled in the high peaks of the Kii peninsula. Nicolas, his French friend, took him to discover the place last year. They first went to Nara, a peaceful city five hundred kilometres from Tōkyō, where Nicolas was giving a lecture at the university. They had stayed two days in a small traditional inn where Nicolas was a regular. The third morning, they went to Osaka where they took a motorcoach to reach Kōya, sixty kilometres further. The rest of the way was in a funicular that took them directly to the Kōya-san site.

There was no hotel or inn around, and most of the visitors went back down at the end of the day. But they could, if they wished, stay for a short time in one of the pilgrimage shelters. The hospitality was kind but austere.

Simon froze the whole night, lying on the ground on a thin, damp straw mat, and the frugal meal had left him hungry.

Nevertheless, he has kept a lasting memory of his experience, which he is unable to put into words, but still comes back to him during his insomnia, when everything is churning inside him and he feel as though he is going to die. It was as though up there, amongst the cedars, cyprus, pines and giant cryptogams in the forest, nine hundred metres in altitude, in the most silent silence and the darkest dark that he has ever experienced, he felt surrounded by something much greater than he was for the first time in his life.

This had nothing to do with the temples he visited during the day, or the multitude of interpretations of the Great Sun Buddha scattered throughout the land, or the precious objects on exposition in the Reihōkan. All these holy commonplaces and sacred treasures only awoke an ethnographic curiosity or aesthetic appreciation in him.

The reclusive monks meditating facing the wall in the small, completely bare rooms had certainly impressed him. Just as the vast necropolis did, where he and Nicolas walked, not daring to speak in the evening mist that rose from the earth between the secular trees already tainted with fawn.

But, these were not the images that came back to him in moments of crisis. It was simply a fleeting yet very real sensation that comforted him without his knowing why.

He had felt a similar emotion a few months later before the great redwood *torii*, standing in the tranquil waters of the Inland Sea, in the Itsukushima marine preserve. The immense, sacred door, composed of vertical pillars and curved transverse beams, flashed in the last rays of sunlight and reflected in the steely blue water. The gigantic structure was cut out from the distant background of mountains already shrouded in shadows and mist.

Simon had already seen hundreds of *torii* at the entrance of the *shintō* temples, symbols of a threshold between the tangible human world and that of the spirits. But he had never felt the least bit moved by this symbolism. This time, on the island Miyajima, the great gate in the middle of the sea seemed to open a passageway before him, onto something unnamed, of which he was vaguely yet undeniably a part.

At nightfall, lanterns were lit throughout the sanctuary where Simon walked for a long time. It was high tide and the long galleries, supported by piles, surrounded the buildings through which the footbridges snaked, leaving Simon with the impression that he was entering some surreal place in the middle of the ocean.

When he took the ferry and had reached Hiroshima by train, he thought of Chloé and the dead trees, still firmly rooted, that she sculpted with a chain saw in the little wood to the left of her house. That place was haunted by a dozen half-starving, stunning characters, dispersed throughout the living. They were different heights, depending on the age of the trees that had been struck by lightening or cracked open by ice.

Simon didn't like walking there because their strange presence made him uneasy, as though he weren't really alone with Chloé in this apparently inoffensive wood. These entities gave off a mysterious force and Simon wished Chloé would cut them down to make a series of sculptures to exhibit in a more conventional place.

When he talked about it, Simon gave the pretext that it was scandalous to let such works be exposed to the bad weather. Really, the fact that these tall, filiform statues were rooted in the earth gave them a kind of life that worried him. He would have preferred to walk amongst them in an art gallery or museum. He wouldn't have felt so threatened by the presence whose power he regarded as stunning, though he feared them where they were.

As soon as he returned to his hotel in Hiroshima, after his visit to the Itsukushima sanctuary, Simon went to bed and fell into a deep sleep. At the end of the night, he had a very peaceful dream in which one of the troubling character's cohorts moved slowly through the water of the Inland Sea, walked through the great marine gate and came to him.

Simon doesn't want to return to the sanctuary for the *O-Bon* because he knows that there will be huge crowds. In the Kōya-san monastery, he'll be able to have a quiet night. He is sure of it. But unlike usual, the effort required for him to organize such a trip seems too difficult and the thought of finding himself in the cities, stations and trains, mixing with the transhuman crowds, discourages him. He decides not to go.

He is also afraid that up there, in that isolated place, he won't be able to get his e-mail. For he must find out as soon as possible, even if it makes him sick, the next part of the story, in which he has just parachuted into the middle of a minefield.

Yesterday, the desire to leave suddenly overcame him, as though Tōkyō were suddenly going to be the target of a bombing and he had to flee, in haste, like the rest of the population. He spent hours on the phone, without ever finding a ticket.

For the last while, Simon hasn't been able to stand his work but, today, he wishes he could keep everyone there and even that he has a busy schedule of meetings imposed on him so he won't have a minute to think.

During his upcoming vacation, he's afraid he'll shut himself in his apartment and lose his mind waiting for the pages that come to him one by one, sometimes with a few days in between.

Kenji gets up and places the report he has finished translating on Simon's desk. Simon must sign it.

Each time it's like he's signing a blank cheque. He has no way of knowing whether Kenji's translation is a faithful representation of his own report. To be sure, Simon would have to hire a second interpreter at his own expense and have the reports Kenji translates into Japanese translated back into English.

The first months, Simon felt this kind of doubt every time he had to sign a document whose content he couldn't verify. Now, he does it without worry, even though he suspects Kenji adds more and more details to the file, as he is less and less able to put them in.

Sometimes during a meeting, Simon gets the impression that Kenji doesn't translate exactly what he says, not out of malevolence — just the opposite — to avoid angry relations with his counterparts.

Instead of being offended, Simon is able to go along with it, but wonders exactly how far this questionable collaboration will go.

As soon as Simon signs his report, Kenji sets some train tickets on his desk.

Simon does not recognize the destination — Mashiko — and he doesn't know why Kenji has set the tickets in front of him. The departure is barely a few hours away.

"*What's that?*" Simon asks him.

"We are going to my father's," Kenji replies in completely remarkable French.

CHAPTER 16

After Simon was born, Gérard was not at all the same with Estelle. He remained as polite as he would be to anyone, but he didn't touch her any more and stopped showing her even the slightest amount of affection. Everything he had imagined about her, albeit falsely, had in the end soiled his image of her, and brought him to decide that it was better to distance himself from this woman if he no longer wanted to feel hurt because of her. But this did not bring the suffering to an end — quite the opposite.

His business was once more in full growth and Gérard spent a lot of time there. He had also started to play golf and cards with some of the suppliers and buyers, and he very often came home late at night, after Estelle had gone to bed. He now slept in the guest room, where he had gradually set up camp.

Except for Simon and Denise, the children were all grown up now and they were off on their respective activities, often outside of the house. Estelle had loved being surrounded by children and mischievous, squawking adolescents. At dinner time, the kitchen and dining room were overflowing with activity.

Gérard, who had always been home very little during the day, had made Estelle the queen of this little kingdom where she had reigned single-handedly over the years. She felt fulfilled in the double role she maintained, as a good mother and perfect wife. She had never confused the two, Gérard wouldn't have allowed it. And even though she often felt torn, she had always given her husband the final say, as her mother had taught her.

It must be said that, despite the principles instilled in her, Estelle wouldn't have acted any differently. She had been so touched by Gérard's worship of her that she would have been willing to make many compromises just to maintain his devotion. For that, she often compromised her own conscience. Among other things, there were times that she didn't defend the children even when she knew that Gérard had gone too far with them. Now, she was upset with herself for not having intervened with the necessary force.

She especially had a hard time forgiving herself for letting Gérard humiliate Claude over all those years. Just as she had allowed him, by not imposing herself on the situation from the beginning, to be pitiless with Denise. Later, Estelle had tried to repair her mistakes, but the harm had already been done and nothing could be changed. She felt like she had failed on all fronts.

Now, the house was almost always empty. Even Denise, who was only an adolescent, was rarely there except to sleep. Still, she had become insolent and dishonest. At times, she would leave without saying where she was going, only returning once she thought she had been worried about. This was often the case at first, but less and less so now. Once, she had spent four days at a friend's parents' cabin without telling them that she hadn't asked permission from her family, who did not know where she was at all. Another time, she had slept in the presbytery gallery after arguing bitterly with her father. Whatever the case, she always found a reason not to be home, especially when Estelle needed her. Denise no longer enjoyed spending time with her mother.

Gérard had completely dropped Estelle. She had lost all privileged status in his eyes, and she felt like she amounted to nothing. She ate dinner alone more and more often after feeding, bathing and rocking Simon to sleep.

This child, so unhoped for, rapidly became the love of her life.

Estelle had loved Gérard, but not the same way he had loved her. She loved Simon to the point of delirium.

Simon had become Estelle's god, and this sweet woman, who had never raised her voice or stated an opinion strongly before, turned easily to fury when it came to defending the interests of her last baby. The child was allowed everything, even the things that had been radically refused to the others — supremacy over their father.

Simon was now the one who slept at Estelle's side in the couple's large bed.

Only he managed to make her laugh in her moments of extreme lassitude or even complete torment.

When Gérard didn't come home at all some nights, or Claude vomited in the entry at three o'clock in the morning and fell asleep at the foot of the stairs, or Denise made a scene and nearly came to blows with her father, or Marie cried for hours at length because she had been left abruptly again, Estelle could not remain indifferent. But she was getting better and better at protecting herself from it all, thinking that everything happening around her was perhaps only a movie, like those she sometimes went to see at the local cinema that occasionally brought her to tears, although they remained exterior to her and, truth be told, didn't concern her.

She would have really preferred to live alone with Simon, and not have to put up with the comings and goings in their house, which always put her at the mercy of others. She could be happy and at peace for hours taking care of Simon, and suddenly someone would burst in and everything would immediately become mysteriously complicated.

Bit by bit, Estelle created a bubble around her and Simon. They lived inside it, she and he, protected from everything that happened "outside," sometimes as little as a few centimetres away.

No one in this house took care of Simon besides Estelle, except Dominique, the rare times she was there. She liked to take him or play with him for a moment, but her heart was elsewhere and with him she dreamt, rather, about the children she would someday have with Christian, the handsome young man she was crazy about.

Simon was an easy child, calm and silent, who seemed to be affected by nothing except his mother's state of mind. Even as a baby, he had been on the lookout for the slightest sign of upset in her. And he had learned how to bring her back to her good mood when she seemed beyond herself, which he could not understand, but knew could not be linked to him because they shared a perfect love.

As soon as Simon started to play with crayons, all his drawings showed that, in his head, the world was divided in two — on one side, there was him and his mother, always carefully drawn, often holding hands, under a big sun; and on the other side, the rest of humanity, represented by a stream of little people, undifferentiated and flat, who looked more like blades of grass than humans.

Gérard had always maintained a certain distance between him and the children, never hesitating to push them away or to give them the impression that they hardly meant anything to him. And for the first time, one of them finally gave him a taste of his own medicine. During Simon's first few years in school, Simon never drew his father into his pictures and never spoke about him in the short descriptions he had to write about his family, though he was penalized for not following his teachers' directions,.

Simon showed such indifference toward Gérard that sometimes he didn't react when his father spoke to him. He continued to play, totally absorbed, as though his father hadn't addressed him. It was to the point where, for a while, Gérard believed that Simon could have been deaf.

But Simon wasn't deaf or blind and he never missed anything that happened around him, even when he seemed not to notice. His favourite pastime was in fact observing, without letting on, the variations in his surroundings, all the undercurrents, however subtle, that went on between people and the deft tactics for survival that each of them had more or less mastered over time.

Simon was particularly observant of Gérard. Something had escaped him — one day, he didn't know where or when — about what was at play between this man, his father, and him. But there had definitely been a major battle, and Simon had come out the winner. He had felt this as a young child.

He didn't have a clear idea about what the causes or the exact stakes had been, but he had no doubt Estelle had something to do with it.

Instinctively, Simon savoured the victory that he had won against his father without having done a thing. And this was not out of vanity or meanness, but because he felt that if the battle had taken place now, he would have certainly been destroyed.

Simon often watched Denise defend herself relentlessly so as not to be chewed up by Gérard. And he knew that he did not have his sister's guts or courage to take on such a giant.

CHAPTER 17

Leaning on a partition, Simon is sitting on the floor, his legs stretched out. His eyes are half-closed. The sake has warmed him and rendered him indolent.

Kenji told him that he could excuse himself, if he wanted to, though no one had left the table yet. Simon had simply preferred to withdraw slightly.

He isn't able to follow the conversation in Japanese but it doesn't matter. He's like a baby snoozing, rocked by the reassuring noise around him, familiar voices and idle movements, pouring the tea slowly into a bowl, setting the lacquered tray on the wooden table, folding paper to form a bird, or quiet footsteps on the *tatami* mats.

The big sliding doors open onto the sheltered gallery overlooking the garden, dim and fresh. The cricket's song mingles with the rustling from inside.

One day Simon discovered, in a boutique in Kyōto, a dozen minuscule bamboo cages, each different from the others. At first he had thought that they were *netsuke*, the ancient miniature artworks still prized and in demand amongst connoisseurs. He had asked the antique shop owner if he was correct: *"Netsuke?"* but the owner replied *"Fol clicket."* Simon asked him to repeat himself. The man then started to imitate a cricket's chirp surprisingly well. Then he repeated *"Clicket."* Simon guessed at the word, incredulous, by correcting the usual Japanese exchange of the *r* for an *l*. *"Cricket? For cricket?"* The man acquiesced, laughing, repeating several times in a high voice, like a child: *"Hai, hai, fol clicket!"* Then he chose the prettiest cage and gave it to Simon, accepting nothing in return.

A few months later, when Nicholas spotted the surprising object at Simon's, he explained to him that in a certain period, people from the big cities would buy small cages like this one with a cricket to set free in their narrow gardens. At night, the cricket's song would lead the city dwellers to believe that, in their suffocating rooms, lying on their damp futons, they were in the country and that a light breeze would soon rise so they could sleep a little.

Simon's thoughts drift softly, peacefully.

Without really knowing why, he feels oddly at ease in this home where family life is coasting along, as though a stranger was not in their midst. He is discreetly taken care of, and nothing is asked of him in return, not even to follow the rules and assume his role as a guest. He just has to be there.

When the train arrived at the station three days ago, around nine o'clock, Simon was so tense that he wanted to leave without even getting out of the train.

Satō Kazumi, Kenji's brother-in-law, came to meet them at the station and take them back to Nogami Kenjirō's house, about fifteen kilometres from the town. Luckily, after introductions were made, the trip was made in silence.

Simon was exhausted and dreading the courteous and fastidious welcome that the family was no doubt going to extend to him. He would certainly be offered the acrid, bitter green tea, probably stored for several hours before in a large electric thermos, as he had so often seen. Then there would be the inevitable, long palaver from which Simon often emerged completely spent.

Yet things had not taken place at all as Simon had anticipated.

Satō Kazumi dropped them off in front of a gate that entered an old farm, and left for Mashiko without any ado.

They walked up to an immense bare wood house with a blue tile roof, surrounded by covered balconies. Kenji's father welcomed them with simplicity, curving himself over and uttering the ritual phrases of welcome. He was alone.

Kenji and Simon took off their shoes in the entry way, Kenji immediately spoke a few words in Japanese to his father, and then wished Simon a restful night.

Then he disappeared down one of the halls to the right.

Disconcerted, Simon followed Nogami Kenjirō across the shadow-steeped dwelling.

The room that had been prepared for him was nearly bare. There was only a futon, covered by a quilt with ashen cranes on a white background, a bedside lamp that was lit and a large terracotta vase set on the floor.

His host then led him down a long passage leading to the Japanese-style bathroom, with steam rising off a deep, fragrant wood bath.

When Simon turned around to thank Nogami Kenjirō, he was gone. Simon was alone as he had so wished.

He lounged at length in the extremely hot water and fell asleep almost as soon as he lay down. But he kept jolting awake throughout the night, looking in vain for his computer. Entire scenes from his past broke over him in gusts inside his head, as though he were continuing, half-awake, a never-ending nightmare. Then, without transition, he would slip again into a restless sleep.

At the first shimmer of dawn, unable to stand it any longer, he pulled on the indigo *yukata* that had been left in the bathroom for him and left his assigned quarters to walk through the sleeping house, trying to calm the unbearable tension inside him.

He couldn't stop shaking, as though a mortal threat was watching his every step. He was having trouble breathing, though the air was warm and sweet. A dense, compact mass was blocking his throat. He was overcome by such a fear of falling that he was certain his whole existence was tumbling through an absolute vacuum.

At the moment he thought he was darkening into an opaque, irremediable state, Kenji said good morning to him in French. Simon resurfaced in one motion and burst into sobs.

From that moment, abandoning the battle, he let himself be carried by what was going on around him.

When Kenji had put the train tickets on Simon's desk in Tōkyō, the only thing he had been worried about, before accepting his interpreter's surprising invitation, was whether there was a computer there, so that he could get his e-mail. Kenji's father didn't have one, but his sister who lived in Mashiko did, and she would bring him his messages each morning if he desired.

But yesterday, when she came, Nobuko didn't mention it — nor did she today. It couldn't be a simple oversight. Simon totally trusts Kenji's word.

Deep down, Simon prefers it like that and doesn't mention it either. For the moment, he doesn't feel up to reading one more line of the painful story that is coming back to him all by itself anyway, and is burning him like an upsurge of lava.

Nobuko bears a strange resemblance to Kenji, though they aren't twins. It is so striking that Simon cannot resist looking often at the brother and sister. They seem like the same being, one simply more feminine and the other simply more masculine. They share the same insight and discretion, which mingles with a calm strength. Passed on from their father, no doubt. And perhaps their mother.

Kenji and Nobuko's mother has died. Simon doesn't know when or why, exactly, but it mustn't be very long past. On the small family altar, next to a lacquered wooden tablet bearing her name in life stands a photograph of her. Nogami Kenjirō and the children gathered there several times, and left a rice cake on a rectangular ceramic plate.

Simon knows that the family members spent several hours at the local cemetery yesterday for *O-Bon*, the festival of spirits. At supper, a place was left at the table for those absent.

When night fell, Simon went with them to the river where they set a few paper boats — a candle in each — onto the water.

He watched the frail vessels follow the current for a moment, then sink one by one as the souls of those disappeared returned to the beyond after a brief visit amongst the living.

CHAPTER 18

Simon slept with Estelle until he was six.

Gérard, who then decided that he was too old to sleep with his mother, awakened him the night before the first day of his first school year.

Simon didn't have time to understand what exactly was going on, just that he ended up alone in a room that was supposed to be his, but had never lived in except for the first eight months of his life.

From Gérard's perspective, he reclaimed their marriage bed on the spot, without any further explanation.

Estelle screamed out loud and with all her might tried to drive the intruder away. They quarrelled for a long time, locked in their room, and Simon didn't miss a word of their argument.

Estelle ended up slamming the door and taking refuge in the guest room.

Simon hoped for hours that she would come and fetch him but it never happened.

He had never had such thoughts before, but that night he wished his father would die during the night, struck by a heart attack as his mother's father had been one year earlier.

But the next morning, Gérard was still alive, though it didn't seem as though he had slept much either.

In the schoolyard, after the ordeal the night before, Simon shook like a leaf, exhausted from a night of insomnia. He was terrorized by the idea of leaving his mother, who cried as though she were going to die during the long, endless hours that separated the two of them for the first time.

When Simon came back to the house after a day that seemed it would never end, all of his belongings had been moved into his new bedroom. Gérard's were scattered around the master bedroom. His mother's robes and dresses were hanging in the guest room closet.

Such an impromptu reordering never took place again, but Simon had concluded that war had once again been declared between him and his father, and that, from the outset, he had lost some important territory.

Estelle made up for that loss, and the loss brought about when Simon started school, by strengthening the bond between them even more. Through this, Simon felt as though he had got some revenge from being thrown brutally from his mother's bed by Gérard.

Simon continued to avoid all direct conflict with his father, but ostentatiously displayed his privileged status in Estelle's heart whenever the occasion permitted. Just to prove that he had not been overcome.

Not only did Gérard refuse to respond to the provocation, he seemed to be interested in Simon as never before in one of his children.

Rather than feeling touched by this, Simon was wary of his father's change in attitude. He grew to believe that his father was planning another horrible surprise for him, like the night he had been driven out.

Every day he came home from school worried, as though Gérard might have killed his mother or made her disappear while he wasn't there. During their dispute, Gérard told Estelle that she had gone completely insane and was turning Simon into a little queer. He told her if she didn't change, he was going to have her locked up.

Estelle was, in fact, growing more and more unstable and she knew it. She could not, however, prevent herself from continually fearing the worst when it came to Simon. Because of that, she refused to let him play the games that all the boys his age were interested in. She was afraid he would fall if he climbed trees, choke if he put a marble in his mouth, drown, catch pneumonia from the slightest cold, get lost, be checked by the bigger boys in hockey, cut himself with the penknife his father had given him, be kidnapped, die from meningitis when he had a headache, be run over in the street, or not wake up one morning. She had fits of hysterics about everything and cried at the slightest thing.

Gérard, though, had never really had the intention of locking Estelle up, despite the fact he sincerely believed she was going too far. And Simon always came home to her after school.

What Simon dreaded the most was exactly what was done to him when classes were over in June, when his suspicion was starting to fade. Without mentioning it to Estelle, Gérard had signed Simon up for summer camp.

At this announcement, Estelle started to holler immediately as though Gérard had just pronounced Simon's death sentence. But this time, Gérard did not let her make a scene. Very quickly, it became clear to Estelle that whatever she did, she would not be able to prevent his departure.

When Estelle went off crying and hid in her room, Simon found himself alone with Gérard in the dining room. They were standing barely a metre apart, facing each other.

Then, amassing all his courage, Simon dared for the first time in his life to stand up to his father, with a barely audible, "I won't go!"

A long silence ensued, during which the petrified Simon was certain his father was going to kill him.

But Gérard, without the faintest aggression, cut straight through his protest, "You'll go. And you'll thank me for it later."

Gérard's decision, despite appearances, had nothing to do with the one he had made years earlier for Denise. He was not trying to get rid of Simon to have his wife to himself. He had lost Estelle forever and he knew that. This time, he felt he was truly acting for his son's benefit. But that wasn't what Simon understood.

Simon contained a rage so violent that it preyed upon him and, that very afternoon, he was stricken by a fever so high that it lasted for over a week, and glands so swollen that he couldn't speak at all.

Estelle tried to take advantage of the situation to turn things around, but as soon as Simon recovered he was off to camp.

The morning of Simon's departure, Estelle had such a migraine that she couldn't stand the smallest sliver of light. When Simon went into her room to kiss her and say good-bye, she held him back, crying, and Gérard had to tear him away from her so that they could leave.

Simon arrived at Saint-Émile five days after the other campers. He'd a hard time fitting in. At first he didn't stop worrying about his mother, whom he had never seen so ill as the moment he had left.

And he felt totally different from the other children, who seemed to be having fun and not to be afraid of anything. He was amongst the tallest and heaviest in his age group, yet he was one of the most timid and awkward. Fortunately this was attributed to his recent sickness and late start with respect to the others.

Gradually, through the patience and kindness of the camp counsellor, and the spontaneous welcome from the other children in his cabin, he began to enjoy certain games, rise to the challenges that he was given, sing with the others around the campfire, be the first to find the markers when they played orienteering games, which he had started to be particularly keen about.

Soon, as though by magic, Simon completely forgot about his mother and became a full-fledged member of the pack, on equal ground with the others.

Simon was so absorbed by all the activities, starting the moment he awoke with a dive into the icy lake water, and only coming to a close the instant he fell asleep, after the inevitable session of whispering that followed lights-out in the cabin, that the end of camp came as a surprise.

Even though he had participated actively, for days in advance, in the preparations for the last day when the parents came to watch various competitions and a few little shows, Simon had not thought about Estelle and Gérard once.

It wasn't until Sunday morning, when Simon saw Gérard arriving alone in the car, without Estelle, that everything came surging back and the reality that he had miraculously escaped for a few weeks caught up with him.

CHAPTER 19

Nobuko is taking Simon and Kenji back to the station for their return to Tōkyō.

They are on the verge of leaving when Nobuko hands a sealed envelope to Simon. She sees Simon's face tense, as though it has been slapped. He knows right away what it is.

He is grateful to the young woman for not having broken the fragile peace that he found here during his stay, by not giving him the envelope earlier. He thanks Nobuko with a bow and slips the envelope into the inside pocket of his jacket. He won't read the pages until he is back in Tōkyō, sheltered in his apartment. If he reads them in the train, he'll worry about losing his self-control again.

Nobuko bows to bid them farewell and wish them a good trip, and it's only at that moment that Simon notices she might be pregnant. He's surprised he hasn't noticed earlier. No doubt because this is the first time he has seen her dressed in western clothing. Nobuko wore *kimono* throughout the *O-Bon*.

Kenji catches Simon's glance and, amused, confirms that Nobuko is in fact expecting a child. On February third. It's very favourable, he explains. This is the date of *Setsubun* festival, the dawn of spring, the ritual of the day is to chase demons from the house to make way for happiness.

Simon congratulates Nobuko, without being able to suppress a slightly sarcastic smile about what Kenji has just told him about February third. The Japanese are very keen about this sort of superstition and ritual. They are sprinkled throughout their daily lives.

Geneviève was born on a February third, twenty years ago. Would it have been enough on that day for Simon to throw a few handfuls of beans around the house for horrible fate to be cast away? And is it because he didn't that the evil spirits came to live in their home?

Simon sometimes resents Kenji, as he does now, for this *naiveté* that lets him say anything: as though everything always works out and shouldn't be worried about, that everything comes in due time, that you just have to patient, burn a few sticks of incense and let things happen.

Outside of his official function, Kenji speaks very little and when he does, it is often this type of prefabricated, sententious phrase that he utters.

Simon knows from having observed Kenji and spending a lot of time with him that these are not empty words for him. But everything seems so simple in this man's life, like magic, that it ends up being irritating.

For Simon too, there was a time when everything was obvious and nothing seemed to be able to resist him. Then, he too could have uttered all those lovely expressions with an air of confidence to anyone.

When he met Sophie, he was twenty-eight and everything was going his way.

After the inheritance he received upon his father's death, he founded his own marketing analysis and strategic planning firm and business took off spectacularly. From the outset, he had the wisdom to find two extremely highly skilled consultants from competitor firms and make them his associates with attractive proposals and legal contracts. As Simon had, they brought several large contracts to the new company. Not to mention the many clients that followed without their suggestion.

Though he wasn't yet thirty, Simon already had undeniable experience in the field. An economics specialist in international business and an MBA graduate from Berkeley, California, he'd had internships in some prestigious marketing companies in the United States and overseas. After his schooling, he worked for three years in Montréal for a multinational corporation. He was also the son of one of Québec's most well-known businessmen. And of course that come to play in the confidence that was bestowed on him, particularly by the banks.

Simon had met Sophie for the first time at his office. She had come to request a market study on a new segment of plastic surgery that would require considerable investment if her clinic decided to get into the field. The type of treatment that the facilities would allow them to offer were extremely expensive for potential customers. He wasn't at all convinced that the demand was great enough for such a project to be profitable over time. Part of the target clientele might prefer to go to the sophisticated New York clinic that had founded the treatment.

Sophie was a plastic surgeon. She was thirty-five and part of a group of six distinguished surgeons.

A major part of their work consisted of reconstructing faces and bodies that had been destroyed or burned, sometimes past the point of recognition. For a single individual, the extent of the work could be so great that the schedule of operations might extend over ten years, without any guarantee ever provided that there would be a gradual reduction in the disgust displayed on others' faces.

The other part of their work — the trivial part — consisted of tiny cuts with the scalpel, minuscule laser projections and a few fine jets of silicone and collagen to improve the images of people inexorably unsatisfied with themselves. In this area, the clinic was a gold mine.

Sophie appealed to Simon from the very first. She was a level-headed, solid and efficient woman. She was so pretty that Simon thought she must have had plastic surgery herself to have such a perfect face. But this wasn't the case. Paradoxically, any surgery on her body terrified her, particularly on her face, even if there had been major flaws. Perhaps it was the fact that she knew exactly what went on in the wings of the operating room. She couldn't bear the idea that while she was under anaesthetic someone would lift the skin covering her face, like a mask, to look underneath and operate.

Three years before they met, she had bought a pretty house in Westmount. Before moving in, she had the place completely redone, including the dishes, tablecloths and bedding, by a designer recommended to her by a friend. After setting a maximum budget, she gave him *carte blanche* provided that he bring out the style of the house, with its old-style mouldings, marble fireplace and oak staircase. She wanted a discreet, refined interior, full of character, but didn't have the time to do it herself. The results were magnificent. Sophie thought the house looked like some of the small hotels where she had stayed during conferences in London.

She spent very little time in the house, though. In fact, the only time she went there was to sleep and on rare occasions to eat. She didn't even like to cook. She had cupboards in the kitchen that she had never opened and would have had quite some difficulty describing what was in them.

Sophie spent most of her time working. When she had any to spare, she went jogging, played squash or went skiing. She liked restaurants, airports, hotels and trips on the fly. She would take an airplane to Toronto, New York or anywhere else to attend a concert or show, and return the next morning on the first flight. Or decide at the last minute to go spend three days in the West Indies. She never took long vacations.

Sophie was exactly the type of woman — and she was a rare breed — that Simon preferred; independent, dynamic and good company. She led her life, he led his, and they saw each other when they could. When it happened, it was always a treat.

Both of them, without really talking openly about it, had gradually tried to make their outings, trips and free time coincide. Sunday mornings, they started to laze around the house in Westmount. More and more often, they would go out for a late-night walk in the city streets. Before going home, they would eat a smoked meat sandwich or *souvlaki* somewhere.

At the time, Simon lived in a huge loft that he rented near his offices on Rue Saint-Paul. But he didn't like the area. He had bought furniture, carpets, lamps and a few pieces of art when he returned from the United States, but they all seemed minuscule and lost in the disproportionate, consuming space.

What Simon hated the most about the place was the noise his footsteps made on the wood floor. One day, when he was walking along the large windows overlooking the port, a memory came back to him. Every morning of Lent until Simon went to school, his mother took him to mass. It would still be dark out. When they would enter the great, empty church and walk up the centre aisle, their footsteps resonated, lugubrious in the cold, damp air. Simon felt a slight dread every time. In the pallid light, he would lean into his mother and when she sat down he sometimes fell asleep in her warmth.

Simon ended up moving in with Sophie. And everything continued smoothly, until Sophie decided one morning that it was time for her to have a child before it was too late. She was thirty-six.

Simon didn't particularly like the idea; he would have gladly given up having an heir, rather than have some little kid come and disturb their lives. But it was important to Sophie.

And she reassured him. Once the child was born, she would hire a nanny to live at the house permanently to take care of the child. It wouldn't change their lives at all.

Sophie wanted a child and she was ready to accept the whole responsibility. Under these conditions Simon agreed to become a parent.

It was also important to Sophie that he officially recognize his paternity and, for that, she also convinced him to marry her if she got pregnant.

As soon as Sophie found out, they married in a very private civil ceremony.

The first two months and the beginning of the third went by as though there were nothing different, without sickness or anything. But as soon as the pregnancy had really become noticeable and actually started to transform Sophie's body, things started to slip — insidiously.

Sophie spent long periods of time naked in front of the large mirrors in the bedroom, examining the deformation of her body, which she could do nothing about. Several times in the beginning, when Simon came across her like this, he went over and started to caress her as he once had. But she would push him away and dress immediately.

Soon, she completely refused for him to see her naked or touch her at all. She often claimed to have a slight migraine that really made her a bit nauseous.

Sophie was usually unable to handle pain or malaise for any amount of time and often overcame such times with whacks of medication. Now that she was pregnant, she was so afraid of giving birth to an unhealthy or freakish child that she didn't dare take anything to crack the deaf pain inside her.

Simon wasn't offended or worried about Sophie's retreat. He told himself that it was probably the normal reaction when a woman was pregnant. In certain animal species, didn't the gravid female leave the male until the birth?

He respected this and moved into the guest room. Then he devoted himself even more to his own activities, never hesitating to leave for a few days, as he had done before when business required him to.

Besides the migraine, which appeared completely bearable, Sophie seemed well. She worked just as hard as ever.

She carefully planned the upcoming months and passed her calendar on to the other surgeons in the clinic. She planned to give up surgery at the beginning of the seventh month, and not take any more appointments in the clinic once she was into her ninth month. She would come back to work three months after the delivery in May.

Her co-workers suggested she stop operating earlier than planned. During the operations, she was often on her feet for long hours, under pressure, and it was very difficult in her condition.

The announcement that Sophie was pregnant took them completely by surprise. They would never have believed that this woman would someday become a mother. They couldn't imagine her bathing a child and humming lullabies to put it to sleep. She always seemed more like the single woman who would go out for a drink alone after a long day's work.

Sophie hid the pregnancy from them for as long as she could, under linen or silk suits with loose jackets. But one day it was obvious. When their astonishment subsided, when they had understood that Sophie was really pregnant and that she was going to be a mother, they started to take care of her and pamper her. Sometimes they tried to lighten her schedule or assign her less demanding operations so it would go unnoticed. One day, Sophie discovered their schemes and flew into a rage of which they would never have thought her capable.

Sophie had such a hard time making a place for herself in this world of men; she put so much extra energy into proving to them that she was as good as any male colleague of the same experience — she wasn't about to lose all that ground because her stomach was getting bigger.

In the clinic and the hospital, she tried to do everything she had before, hiding her fatigue under makeup. She also took on, when necessary, the grand airs of a woman in bloom — re-creating the world inside her, as though there were nothing to it.

But when she went home and learned that Simon would be coming home late or in two or three days, she fell into a living room chair and let herself slip, without holding back, into a deep depression. She could stay there for several hours, crying and wanting to die.

To save face, even in front of Simon, Sophie did everything despite her physical and mental exhaustion to follow the exact programme she had set for herself prior to the birth. She had managed to restrain her waves of worry and anxiety that often bordered on total panic, so that she only exploded during her time alone.

The delivery was extremely difficult. Labour lasted for sixteen hours. Sophie didn't want Simon there. She refused to let him see her that way, completely undone by a pain from which she had no respite.

Simon waited in the private room reserved for his wife. He was able to work there quietly, until Sophie finally managed to expel the child.

CHAPTER 20

When Simon saw that Estelle wasn't with Gérard, he acted as though he hadn't seen his father's car arrive at the camp, and went to hide in the woods on top of an embankment.

From there, he watched the arrival of the other parents and his friends' reunion with their fathers and mothers, and often their brothers and sisters.

He saw Gérard looking for him, in the cabin, in the big teepee, by the canoes, in the cafeteria, everywhere.

Simon felt like a limp rag. His knees were shaking. His mouth was dry and he couldn't breathe.

He stayed there for nearly an hour, crouched over, being bitten by insects in the humid July air.

He didn't come back down from his observation point until the call to assembly that marked the beginning of the festivities. The parents were seated on folding chairs arranged on the grass.

Simon avoided looking in their direction. He was afraid if he met his father's gaze, he wouldn't be able to participate in the activities and would be a weakness to his cabin in the various competitions.

At the same time, he was afraid his father had left. Perhaps to get even. Or simply because he thought his son wasn't at the camp. That he must be in the wrong place. That maybe he didn't even have a son.

Under the blazing sun, Simon tormented himself into fainting right in the middle of the director's speech.

When Simon came to in the infirmary, he saw Gérard leaning over him, worried. He asked right away where his mother was. Gérard took his hand and promised him that she was well, very well even, but couldn't be there.

Simon didn't believe him. He jerked back his hand, as though it had been burned, and got up saying that he wanted to go home.

They wanted him to take more time to recover, but Simon had only one thing in mind: to go home and see for himself.

All the way back to the city, Gérard sought the words to reassure Simon and explain what had happened while he had been away. He had been preparing for this for days, trying to find a way to explain so Simon didn't close up like an oyster. Because that's what Gérard expected, for Simon to grow totally inaccessible and cold, hard as stone, walled inside his apparent impassivity. But this time, Simon huddled against the door, crying silently, and Gérard didn't know what to say.

The instant they arrived, Simon hurried in and ran around the house calling for his mother.

In the bathroom, he found himself facing Denise, who had just brushed her teeth. In a flash, she recognized all the disarray Simon was feeling and said immediately to calm him, "She's fine! Simon, she's fine!"

By then Gérard had appeared in the hallway, but Denise shut the bathroom door on him.

She was the one to tell Simon what had happened, skipping a lot of facts and considerably attenuating the seriousness of the situation. Simon wasn't crying anymore. He listened to Denise without blinking, totally shattered.

When she finished, Simon said in a faint voice, "I want to see her."

Simon didn't give up for three days. He remained seated in the living room, repeating that same phrase every time anyone said anything to him.

At that time, children weren't allowed into hospitals and Gérard didn't see how he could calm Simon's worry. He spoke with the psychiatrist treating Estelle, who deemed it desirable indeed for Simon to have a short visit with his mother. However, this could not take place just any way or time. A time would have to be chosen when Estelle was well enough for Simon to be reassured by seeing her, not the opposite.

In the long hallways that led to Estelle's room, Simon was sure life would be able to continue in a few minutes; the very moment he finally had his mother back.

Gérard pushed open a door and they entered a room where Simon saw a very thin woman, with a sallow face and faded hair, sunken into a chair that seemed to be trying to swallow her up.

Simon thought they were in the wrong room and he started to leave when he heard a familiar voice calling him from behind.

As soon as Simon realized the woman he hadn't recognized was his mother, the world crumbled beneath him. At that very moment, Simon was taken by the conviction that everything that had happened to his mother during his absence was his fault because he had totally abandoned and forgotten her. At the same time, he cursed his father who had not only allowed, but actually arranged, for such a thing to happen.

After Simon's departure for summer camp, Estelle quickly sank into a deep depression. She spent a lot of time resting, often in one of the living room chairs or in Simon's room, and she didn't even go to the trouble of getting dressed in the morning. She dragged about the house wrapped in a chenille housecoat completely out of season.

She didn't answer the telephone anymore and Gérard was so worried about her he came home every day at lunch to make sure everything was all right. Nothing was all right, but he would go back to work anyway, slightly reassured that she was still alive.

Often the whole house was steeped in shadows in the middle of the day. Estelle would be sitting at the kitchen table, her head in her hands, crying or absorbed in her private thoughts.

When Gérard came into the kitchen and found Estelle like that, it was the nape of her neck that he first noticed, bare beneath the wobbly chignon that she now carelessly made without bothering to look at herself in the mirror.

Each time Gérard felt like crying with her. He would have given anything to erase the implacable time that had run on from the moment when, almost exactly thirty years before, he had looked at this very same nape and the wildest dreams were theirs, to the point where they were now, where everything was ruined. He would have given anything to go back and prevent this dreadful waste of their lives.

In the eyes of many, Gérard was a winner, the sort of man who had succeeded at everything. In business, he had unparalleled wisdom and rare intuition, never hesitating to try out new avenues that no one dared explore, getting out quickly the moment he suffered a setback.

He had a delectable wife, who made him the envy of many men, and a lovely, close family, even though the eldest had been living in Vancouver for three years. This departure hadn't shocked anyone because Gérard was the one who had given the children a taste for travel by taking them to several countries while they were very young.

What people didn't know was that Claude left to live on the other side of the world, away from his father, to enjoy his life in peace.

Just as they didn't know that the handsome, rich prince that Marie had ended up marrying was actually an old sex maniac, only in love with her young ass, which he often placed as a bet during poker games with his friends.

Dominique seemed to be the most well-balanced, and she was, but that had come at the high cost of constant effort to build herself a life with Christian, away from the tensions in the big house on Rue Saint-Denis. She always felt exhausted, however, in spite of her hearty constitution, as though there were hidden cracks in her, from which her energy continually escaped in very fine trickles.

Denise, however, was her father's daughter, passing for a young, ambitious woman, which explained the tension that still reigned between them, though diminished considerably. Unlike Dominique and Marie, Denise had wanted to pursue higher education in an area that was still strictly reserved for men. In fact, she liked being considered as a man, even by women, whom she often desired.

Under his elegant polish and behind his apparent success, Gérard had dragged Estelle and the children into a pit of quicksand, where they were fighting and sinking — each one of them — some more slowly than others.

In fact Gérard had never really contemplated until now the scope of the disaster he had insidiously created over time, with his silence and manner of keeping a barely noticeable distance and his attitude that gave every one of them a subtle yet sinister impression of always being in the way or, worse yet, of not really existing at all.

When Gérard finally realized, seeing Estelle's relentless attempt to prevent the same thing happening to Simon, it was too late.

Now she was the one, who, wanting to do the right thing, went too far — nearly forcing the child she believed she was protecting to the brink of a chasm as great as the one she wanted to save him from.

Gérard only came to realize all of this gradually, over the time he had given up on Estelle and as the battle he had waged over the years against his own children came to a natural end.

Evaluating the extent of the damage, he had at least hoped to pull Simon out of the mire by using extreme measures to distance him from his mother. But the more Estelle sank into depression, the more Gérard believed that Simon would inevitably drown with her.

When Gérard came to the house at lunch hour, he tried many ways to get Estelle, who was getting thinner by the day, to eat a bit. But she would only drink large glasses of milk that she gulped down all at once, making a face as though she were trying to get rid of them, leaving her with a moustache that she didn't wipe off. If Gérard tried, she wailed mutedly and pushed him away.

For two weeks, Estelle completely stopped speaking.

One night when he came home, Gérard found her on the floor in the bathroom, wrists slashed open. She was moaning, curled up in a ball on the little mat, and covered in blood. This time, though he felt he was brushing against a despair that was certainly more tragic than when she fell down the stairs, he stayed in control of himself and did what had to be done. He called an ambulance immediately and had her taken to the hospital emergency ward.

The wounds were deep and the tendons were cleanly sliced by a razor blade, but Estelle hadn't cut any major veins and her life had not been in danger.

After suturing and dressing her wounds, she was transferred to the psychiatric ward where she spent three months.

When she was finally released, one Wednesday in September, the woman that Gérard brought home was no longer totally ravaged like the one Simon had seen in the hospital at the end of July.

But she wasn't his mother either. Her dresses didn't fit her. They floated over her spindly body. At her gaping neckline, her collarbone jutted out, just like the top of her breastbone and ribs. Where her breasts had once been, where Simon had cuddled so many times and liked to follow the light movement of his mother's breath, that place was flat, lifeless. The clothing yawned, with nothing inside it.

CHAPTER 21

This morning, Simon didn't go to work. He asked Kenji to tell Miki Yoshitaka that he is ill and doesn't know when he will return. Kenji can invent whatever he thinks is suitable to excuse Simon.

The pages he received in Mashiko and since his return are unbearable. This story is killing him.

He doesn't know how he'll manage to escape the violence of the memories that are coming back and exploding incessantly in his head.

Inside him, they're stirring and superimposing on one another. Links are forming between pieces of his life that had always seemed totally disconnected from one another. Between people so different that it seemed impossible to make any connection between them — before.

The image of his mother, sitting in a beige vinyl chair in the hospital, comes back to him, intact. He remembers the slightest details. The odour of urine in the room. The raw July light that mercilessly struck his mother's face, accentuating its lividity. The noise her dentures made when she spoke to him. She grew so thin that they floated in her mouth, which was dry from the medication. Her breath was fetid. He had noticed even from a distance. When she had tried to kiss him just before he left, he had turned quickly and his mother's lips had only brushed his ear. Then Simon left without turning back.

Inside Simon's head, another scene has grafted itself to this one and they've become so fused sometimes he has the impression they involve the same woman, which is not at all true.

Simon is thirty. He has been asked to come to the hospital quickly. A doctor comes to meet him at the main entrance as soon as he arrived. On the way, the doctor talks to Simon and explains what is happening. Simon doesn't hear him. Since they started, he has been counting the doors on the left and right of the long corridors they're walking down. The doctor walks too fast and talks too much. Simon has to make a real effort not to be distracted. His entire body is trembling.

Simon is brought into a supervised area where there are only five rooms, with maximum security.

They stop before a closed door. On the other side, a woman is yelling out swear words and insults. Simon knows this voice.

The doctor says: "It seems really terrible now but everything will come back to order. It passes."

The doctor opens the door to the room.

Simon sees a wild woman who abruptly lifts her head from the pillow to spit in his direction and swear at him. Leather straps restrain her wrists and ankles to the bars of the bed, which she is shaking violently.

The doctor closes the door.

Two days after Geneviève's birth, Sophie fell into a postpartum depression. When Simon saw her she was in peak crisis.

Simon only returned to visit Sophie once while she was in the hospital. She asked to see him. She had just come out of her delirium. She was in such a depression and under the influence of so much medication she had trouble speaking. But she was lucid.

She made Simon promise not to come back until the day she was released, even though it could be months. And she made him swear that he would take care of their daughter while she was getting better. Afterwards, she wouldn't ask him for anything else.

Simon promised he would.

Their meeting had barely lasted three minutes. Sophie was physically unrecognizable. It looked as though she had barely escaped from a serious attack that had almost claimed her.

Before he took Geneviève home with him, the nurses in the nursery helped him to find someone reliable to take care of the baby. But the woman, Madame Potvin, mother of six children and grandmother of eight, could only be there from seven in the morning to seven at night. And, she would take Sunday off. The rest of the time, Simon would be responsible for the child.

The first few hours Simon found himself alone with Geneviève, he was at such a loss that he didn't know what to do when she awoke and started crying. He left her in her *couchette* and paced the house, swearing and wondering aloud how he let himself be dragged into such a mess.

The first night, Simon went to bed exhausted and slept deeply without stirring until morning.

When Madame Potvin arrived, she gave him a lecture for not taking proper care of Geneviève. He didn't change her diaper or feed her. The bottles were ready. He just had to warm them up a little. It wasn't that complicated!

The next night, Simon made a little enclosure in his bed with pillows, so Geneviève could sleep with him. If she cried, he would hear her. He also set his alarm clock so he wouldn't miss her feeding times.

Very soon, he understood the pattern of the essential responsibilities.

And gradually he started to hold Geneviève and carry her around the house, propped against his shoulder. Sometimes when she had long fallen asleep, though he knew it, he continued to walk gently with her.

Geneviève was not a difficult child and as soon as he took care of her a little, she gave herself up to him. Sometimes, Simon was so touched it brought tears to his eyes.

Simon's whole life had changed. He was anxious to come home in the evenings and Sundays became days to celebrate.

Then one day, Sophie was released from the hospital.

Her return was difficult. Sophie no longer felt at home in the house where Madame Potvin knew more about where things were, what had to be done, and when to do them for Geneviève.

In the evenings and on Sunday when Madame Potvin was off, Simon took control and oversaw things. This astonished Sophie. He, who had never wanted a child, was a perfect father.

During the previous month, Madame Potvin had taken Geneviève to the hospital to see Sophie. At first, she only stayed a few minutes.

Progressively, a relationship grew between mother and daughter and Sophie spent hours with Geneviève, taking care of her and rocking her.

But it all seemed like a game and, when Sophie had enough, she put Geneviève back in Madame Potvin's arms to be taken away.

It was like a game at home, too. Madame Potvin and Simon left her to take care of Geneviève for awhile, watching from the corners of their eyes, ready to come and help.

She was never left at home alone with Geneviève and was treated like a major invalid, who couldn't be relied upon even for small things.

When Simon sneaked a glance at Sophie, he couldn't help himself from thinking that she was a broken woman. She had lost all her confidence. She was often demoralized and cried at times for no apparent reason. She was no longer the woman he had loved. She had no spirit any more, no panache.

Yet, at this time, the idea of leaving her would never have crossed his mind. Because of Geneviève. What he was discovering with her was so simple and sweet that all the rest had become secondary.

It had been like that for more than a month.

Then one night, Sophie had raised her voice in front of Geneviève when Simon had insisted on giving his daughter the eardrops for her infection himself.

Simon had given her such a look that Sophie retreated immediately. There was something in his eyes Sophie was unable to understand, but had hurt her deeply.

In the days that followed, Sophie lost her temper again several times with Simon, and with Madame Potvin.

In a moment of impatience, Simon ended up letting an "I hope this isn't going to start again!" slip out, but loudly enough for Sophie to hear.

This time, Sophie exploded. She had started screaming and broke a vase in the living room.

She found herself promptly in the hospital emergency ward, where they tried to give her an injection to calm her down. But the more they tried to restrain her, the harder she fought back. They had ended up strapping her to a bed again and giving her a tranquilizer.

Watching her, Simon was sure that the fury he had seen a few months earlier in the room on the third floor had returned.

But it was just Sophie coming back to herself.

When the psychiatrist arrived, he spoke with Sophie for a long time, one to one.

He untied a sobbing Sophie.

The psychiatrist then brought Simon into a small consultation room. He first explained that Sophie was going to stay at the hospital until the next morning because of the tranquilizer they had injected. Then he began to talk to Simon about Sophie.

Except for the first two weeks of Sophie's serious crisis, after the birth, Simon had never met with her psychiatrist. She wanted it like that, because she was ashamed of what was happening to her.

The psychiatrist explained to him that Sophie was no longer in psychosis, but that she would have to work very hard at repairing her relationship with her daughter. Though Sophie considered herself an excellent surgeon, she felt incompetent in her new role as a mother, as many women did indeed. Sophie was probably facing the greatest challenge of her life. She needed free rein. Let her gradually experience being a mother. Leave her alone more and more often with Geneviève. Have confidence in her.

Simon had retorted that he was afraid for Geneviève. Sophie was fragile. The smallest thing tired her out. Now she flew off the handle for everything. She could be impatient with Geneviève, yell, let her cry for hours in her *couchette*, forget to feed her.

The psychiatrist answered, "That could certainly happen. It's the risk that must be taken so that Geneviève has a mother."

Simon left the meeting completely upset and angry. For this man, his patient's healing appeared to count for more than Geneviève's safety and well-being.

Simon also found it difficult not to feel accused of monopolizing their daughter and preventing Sophie from coming into contact with her. In truth, he was made to feel responsible for the fact that she hadn't succeeded in being a mother.

In the weeks to come, Simon gradually effaced himself in a fit of pique, leaving more responsibility to his wife. As the psychiatrist had predicted, over the months, she had succeeded in developing a real bond with her daughter.

After a year, Sophie had recovered completely. She had gradually gone back to work as a plastic surgeon, while still making time for Geneviève. It had become a priority for her. She didn't want to bury herself in work as she once had.

She also would have liked to spend more time with Simon, and, though she often asked him, he was more and more involved with his work. He even went overseas frequently.

After three years, Simon had left the house for good.

Geneviève had lost a father.

CHAPTER 22

For several years, Simon tried desperately to bring his mother back to what she had been before the fateful summer he had lost her, but it was a superhuman undertaking.

Estelle had nevertheless improved a lot in the meantime. In appearance, for those who didn't know her intimately, she had nearly become her old self, as she was before Simon's birth, calm and laughing.

But inside there was something different about her. When she laughed she had the wind in her voice. And there was an absent look in her eye. When Simon looked into her eyes, he felt as though she didn't really see him or that she wasn't quite there. He even thought sometimes that she purposely drew a veil over what was happening inside her so that he couldn't reach it.

There were now great open spaces in her, a cushy, uninhabited world where she liked to seek refuge and let herself go with nothing to stop her, sheltered from everything on the outside that hurt. It was like the ocean where she had always so loved to float for hours on her back, a short distance from the others, warming in the sun. Now when she was about to wash up on painful shores, she took a tranquilizer and gently floated out to sea.

Despite his effort, Simon was never able to reach her as he might have wished, that is, reach her completely, as he could before.

And that was what she wanted, even if she was obliged to flee far away, inside herself, to avoid witnessing the distress she saw in him. She had to constantly remind herself that she was doing it for him, in spite of appearances.

Until the age of twelve, Simon had held out against his father without yelling or causing a scene, though unshakeable in his mute obstinacy every time his father tried to distance him from his mother. He did not go back to summer camp and he did not board in *collège*, as his father would have liked. He didn't even agree to go to stay with Dominique, who now lived in Québec with Christian and their two young children. He didn't leave his mother unless Estelle decided to leave, without him, to stay with one of her sisters.

It was during one of her absences, which lasted nearly a month, that Simon started to grow away from his mother. It was the beginning of the summer and so as not to leave Simon at home alone, Gérard decided to take him to the office and put him to work a little. He proposed a sort of proper contract — official — as he might have drawn up with anyone. And that is what led Simon to accept, without feeling trapped by his father.

From the moment when Simon came back from camp and found his mother in the hospital in a completely pitiful state, the rapport between father and son grew so glacial that even Gérard, truly a specialist in icy wars, suffered. He even tried a number of different ways to get close to Simon — in vain.

Knowing Simon's attachment to his mother, Gérard completely devoted himself to taking care of Estelle during her long convalescence. He remained affectionate toward her afterwards, all the while maintaining a respectful distance.

The solicitude that Gérard showed toward Estelle was anything but feigned. Quite the opposite. He slowly found the love again that he had always had inside him for Estelle, though finally stripped of everything that was destructive and stifling.

Simon couldn't understand such a turnaround, which seemed hypocritical and suspicious to him. Until then, he had never seen Gérard display any sign of affection toward Estelle. And because of his parents' many quarrels, Simon had come to believe that his father not only hated his mother, but that he must have also secretly wished she was dead.

Simon didn't understand anything about what went on around him anymore. Especially since his mother's attitude was equally out of the ordinary.

Estelle no longer showed any hostility toward Gérard and she didn't check any of his awkward but sincere attempts to finally make peace, simply, for all the difficulties they had gone through. Without seeming to do anything on her part to provoke a reconciliation, she didn't object to Gérard's approaches. And it was undeniable that she was touched by the tenderness in him, which she thought had disappeared forever. She didn't say anything about it and tried not to let on, but Gérard didn't miss it.

Simon didn't miss it either, but preferred to believe his mother was not only indifferent to his father's attention, but that it irritated her more often than not. She would discreetly try to suppress a smile when, according to Simon, Gérard was overdoing it, and Simon told himself that she had to hold herself back to avoid laughing in her husband's face. Because, in Simon's eyes, she must have despised how reluctant he was, which Gérard sometimes seemed to be when he was trying to be nice.

If she had been able, Estelle really would have liked to return the affection Gérard had started to show toward her, but something had broken inside her. Sometimes at night, as she lay at his side and he had fallen asleep touching her, barely, sometimes just the tips of his fingers, she told herself that one night she would be able to move closer to him and fall asleep, like before, such a long time ago, with her head on his shoulder. But she wasn't able to yet.

That summer, Gérard thought that things were changing between him and his son when Simon showed a noticeable interest in what was happening in his business.

His fascination was such that, even when Estelle came home in the middle of July, Simon asked Gérard to extend his contract until school started. Gérard agreed, happy to see Simon finally make a move away from his mother.

In fact, Simon had hesitated before asking such a thing from his father because he was afraid that Estelle would feel abandoned, but he really wanted to continue working.

And, Estelle didn't seem to suffer the absence of her son for the remainder of the summer. When Simon came home, sometimes late, with Gérard, his mother was no worse or better than if he were to have spent the day playing cards with her or strolling through the stores, museums and parks, or if they had gone to the cinema. Though he was the one who had decided not to stay with her, at first, Simon missed her deeply.

One evening, the house was empty when they came home, something that had not happened since Estelle had been in the hospital. She had left them a note saying that dinner was in the refrigerator and that she had gone to the theatre with a friend. Simon felt so angry that he went to his room without eating.

When he heard her come in at one in the morning, he swore that from that point on his mother would have to get along without him, since she no longer seemed to need him around.

At the end of the summer, his resentment had dissipated as though by a miracle, leaving him with a strange feeling of relief that surprised him. He didn't know quite what to do about it.

His father had enrolled him in a *collège classique*, well-known for its education and extracurricular activities. When the year began, Simon enrolled for the first time in several activities. And when his father worked on Saturdays, Simon asked if he could go along. And Gérard never refused.

Simon was very successful in his first year, only hoping to please his mother. The importance he placed on being first in his class wasn't out of ambition, but so that she would be proud of him.

From the moment he started basic Latin, everything changed. Marks, report cards and what his mother thought didn't matter much to him, as he developed a true passion for everything that concerned humanity, history, beliefs and life in society. Everything interested him and he felt that he had a lot to catch up on, as though he hadn't really existed until then. He spent all his free time reading. A world was opening before him, a world he hadn't known until then because he had been enclosed in a bubble with his mother.

He gradually became so enthralled in everything he was discovering that he totally forgot Estelle's existence, again.

When she died, in a silly accident one Sunday afternoon in February on the highway to the north where she had gone on an outing with her sister, Simon hardly felt a thing and did not weep. As though his mother had died several years earlier and he had already grieved for her.

Her death damaged him, however, to a point where he would fall to complete ruin if he let it wholly invade his consciousness.

As soon as he felt the sobs rising inside his throat, he strangled them and short-circuited his pain by counting anything that came into his head — the wolves on his bedroom wallpaper, the number of cars they passed in the street, the words on a box of cereal, his own steps, or the blinking of his eyes — sometimes for hours at a time.

Estelle's coffin was closed. Simon could not see his mother for the last time. At the funeral, people whispered that her face had been completely crushed in the accident, and that there was nothing left except a mass of flesh and bones that could have been anyone or anything. Except Simon's mother.

CHAPTER 23

Simon is lying in his room in Mashiko. He feels completely empty.

Three weeks ago in Tōkyō, when Nicolas discovered the prostrate state into which Simon had plunged, he insisted that Simon agree to let one of his friends, a doctor, come to see him.

Simon ended up consenting to the consultation simply because he needed a medical certificate to justify his long absence from work. But as soon as the doctor started to make him talk about what was not right, Simon burst into tears and something fissured inside him.

In ten days, Simon has seen the doctor four times.

Because the mental anguish tearing him apart is atrocious and because he feels in danger, Simon has agreed to take antidepressants. Yet, he has refused to return to Québec as the doctor suggested. For now, he is unable to.

Instead, he has asked Kenji if he can return to Mashiko until things settle down a bit inside him.

Here, alone with Kenji's father, who speaks only Japanese and who quietly sees to his business without asking anything of him, Simon can safely let himself go.

In fact, besides sleeping and eating what Nogami Kenjirō puts in front of him at meal time in a constellation of small ceramic bowls, Simon does nothing. He stays lying on his *futon* or leaning against one of the partitions in the dining room. Or sits on a rock in the garden, watching the fine trickle of water run down a bamboo stalk and lose itself in the thick moss a few centimetres below.

At certain moments, it seems as though there isn't anyone inside him. Simon watches the trickle of water run, and that is all. Sometimes for hours at a time.

At other moments, such painful thoughts and emotions run through him that he moans quietly. But he doesn't fight them anymore.

He simply waits for them to pass. And they always end up passing, even if it sometimes takes a while.

Afterwards he sleeps — exhausted.

When he awakens it's calmer inside him. He can then look at things from the outside and let himself absorb them.

Nobuko comes to the house every morning, very early. She often brings meals that she has prepared for her father and Simon. She never stays very long. She is always dressed in western clothing and her pregnancy is now obvious.

Simon never asks her if she has received any mail over the Internet for him. He wouldn't read it anyway.

Nogami Kenjirō is eight years older than Simon. If Kenji hadn't told him this during his first visit, Simon wouldn't have known. He has trouble guessing the age of Japanese people. And with Simon in his current state, Nogami Kenjirō almost seems younger.

Yet, in spite of their age and all logic, Simon cannot help but see a father in this man. Not Simon's father, but a father nevertheless.

Gérard wasn't like Nogami Kenjirō at all.

Except in business, Simon's father had always been tense, worried. As though, behind what was visible, there was something else, dire, against which he had to fight constantly. And even when he made every effort he always ended up losing the invisible battle, in which he couldn't even see his opponent.

After Estelle's death, Gérard had gone through a very difficult period. Though he had begun to hope that he would be able to regain her bit by bit and find a sort of peace with her, the death of his wife had left him completely alone with his pain and remorse.

He sold the house first, which was too full of history, and moved with Simon into a luxurious but totally impersonal apartment building near Mont Royal.

Strangely, what later helped Gérard come back to life was that his son Simon was more and more interested in his business.

Their relations had been cold and they never spoke, except in cases of extreme necessity, but Gérard interpreted Simon's interest in what he had spent his entire life building as an undeniable mark of his esteem. His son couldn't say it, Gérard understood these things, but it was obvious.

And it became all the more obvious to him when Simon announced he was enrolling in business school.

To show Simon how touched he was, Gérard had rented him an apartment near the university and bought him a car.

When he wasn't studying, Simon continued to work for his father, and Gérard had gradually become convinced that he had found a successor.

Gérard was in his sixties. He wasn't at all ready to retire, he adored working and wouldn't have known what else to do, but was prepared to pass the reins to his son, little by little, once he had finished his studies.

After his Bachelor's degree, Simon had decided to do a Master's at Berkeley. Not only did Gérard see no problem with this decision, he thought that with all the knowledge Simon would bring back, they could push the business even further ahead — together.

Gérard was so proud of his son that he spoke openly of him as his heir apparent, without Simon's knowing.

When Simon came back from California, having graduated with honours from one of the most prestigious universities in America and gained rich in experience from numerous corporate internships, Gérard organized a great celebration.

But at the end of the meal, after officially offering Simon partnership in the company, Gérard was disappointed.

Simon had never had the intention, once he received his diploma, to work with his father. Incontestably, Gérard had been Simon's mentor, he was able to recognize, but he was only interested in marketing, nothing else. Especially not the manufacture and sales of life enzymes that were supposed to clean the body and restore its youth, or vials to drink, apparently capable of increasing virility tenfold. While studying at Berkeley, a major Montréal marketing firm had approached him and already hired him, for his return.

After the celebration dinner, which had turned to disaster, Simon had cut off all ties with his family.

A year and a half later, Denise went to see him because Gérard had just learned that he had liver cancer. He didn't have long to live.

Denise had left her job in a pharmaceutical company to take over her father's business when he had started to lose interest in it, a few months after Simon's return. Gérard had grown depressed and spoke of selling the company. In his eyes, all the ingenuity and tenacity that he had shown throughout his life to build an empire, had been for nothing. Gérard had even told Denise that he thought he had failed, just like his eldest son Claude, found frozen in a park in New York, four years earlier.

Simon had waited as long as possible before going to see his father in the hospital.

When Simon came into his room, Gérard was dying but perfectly coherent.

Gérard had asked Simon's forgiveness for all the hurt he had caused him. He spoke a lot about Estelle. And he had tried to explain certain things about the past to him, things he had taken too long to understand himself.

But at the time Simon could not listen. He had kept his father's words under protective seals, because the pain they awoke in him was too much to bear.

CHAPTER 24

Sometimes Nobuko arrives with e-mail for Simon.

Chloé has started to write to him again. She tells him about what she is painting, about the renovations she is gradually having done in her house, about the *Bouvier des Flandres* she adopted.

A few weeks after they met, Simon tried to convince Chloé to get a watchdog. He thought it unwise that she lived in such isolation without protection. He brought the subject up often.

Chloé, on the other hand, preferred to wait because she had an old, stormy, grey tomcat that was scared stiff of dogs.

To Simon, Chloé's safety was much more important than this fourteen-year-old cat, who would die soon anyway.

One day, believing she would give in once it was done, he arrived at her house in a small truck with an enormous kennel and a young Doberman that he'd had trained for her.

As soon as they arrived, Simon, the dog and the kennel found themselves back on the road again, going the opposite way.

Simon hasn't written to Chloé yet. He isn't ready. But he likes that she tells him about herself, simply, without asking him a single question and without re-opening the old discussions that lead nowhere.

Simon has been in Mashiko nearly two months now and he is gradually getting back on his feet.

This morning it's raining. Leaning against the bark of one of the trunks supporting the balcony's overhang, Simon listens to the rain fall. The scents of the foggy garden mingle with the odour of cut straw coming from inside, where the old *tatami* have been replaced with new ones, in certain rooms, like every year.Nogami Kenjirō's house calms Simon. It only has one floor and no cellar, attic or nooks.

With its sliding doors — the *shōji* and *fusuma* — all of the rooms can open, as desired, onto one another and to the outside. Between the inside and the outside there is no clear boundary.

In this house, it seems that all the space is kept empty. The rooms are large and bare, and there are few objects.

Only the large terra-cotta vases are set on the floor, here and there, on the balconies, in the house and even in the slightly wild garden surrounding it. On the other side of the pond, the water arriving from a stream runs into large stone basins that overflow, one into the other, with a light lapping sound into the natural pool.

Nogami Kenjirō is a potter. His workshop is located in a nearby building connected to the main house by a sheltered footbridge on piles. As soon as he goes there in the morning, he slides all the *shōji* open, even when it's cool outside.

The first three weeks, Simon would sit not far from there, on the wooden footbridge, to watch Nogami Kenjirō work.

He kneads a piece of clay for a long time before throwing it onto the centre of the disc of the potter's wheel, which he turns with his feet. Then shortly, as if by magic in the hands of Nogami Kenjirō, from the compact mass of wet earth rises a teacup, a jar, an incense dish or a bowl. Simon loves the moment when the form surges forth, as well as the patient finishing work that follows.

One day, the potter brings Simon into his workshop and places him without a word in front of a large piece of clay.

Simon doesn't know what Nogami Kenjirō expects from him, exactly. He doesn't feel like trying it out at all. Watching from a distance is enough. But Nogami Kenjirō stands behind him, places Simon's hands inside his, and plunges them into a bowl of water before sliding them slowly over the wet clay.

Then Nogami Kenjirō goes back to his work, leaving Simon alone, his hands on the cold, sticky surface.

The potter turns his back to Simon and starts painting subtle vegetable patterns on biscuit-shaped pieces, over a base of yellowish ochre and other washes pigmented with mute colours.

Simon remains motionless for a long moment, repressing what is swelling up inside him. He is boiling with anger. What right does Nogami Kenjirō have to impose such contact on him?

Not daring to show his displeasure to Kenji's father, Simon pushes his fingers deep into the clay, which he begins to knead in rage.

The next morning he comes to sit in the same spot.

Since then, Simon often comes to play with the earth, kneading and moulding it with his hands. Among other things, he has shaped several little statues between ten and twenty centimetres tall, which look like Chloé's sculptures in her haunted forest and the ones in the dream he had, not far from the Itsukushima marine preserve.

Nogami Kenjirō has put the little statues in the middle of his own pieces, in a wood oven he only rarely fires and that is built into the embankment near the pond. After twenty minutes, he takes them from the oven with long tongs and lays them, incandescent, in a large receptacle full of dead leaves, rice straw and cedar shavings that catch flame instantly. Then he plunges them into a basin of water that boils for a brief moment.

They are now standing on the floor in Simon's room. Each one is different in its form and colour, even though they are all covered in the same matte glaze. On some of them, the grey-green is dominant, on others, it's the coppery red that comes out. One is sprinkled with gold in places. Another is almost turquoise. The fire left its mark on every one of them in a different way. Together, they form a strange cohort that seems to watch over Simon as he sleeps.

Usually Nogami Kenjirō only lights one of his ovens about once a month. As soon as he has finished a firing, Nobuko comes to get the new pieces.

Simon learned only recently that Nogami Kenjirō's work is very much in demand, both in Japan and abroad. Nobuko and Kenji have the exclusive rights of sale. Nobuko has a boutique in Mashiko, where she takes care of their distribution to several locations in Tōkyō, Nara and Kyōto, and their export.

Simon has trouble understanding how such simple, austere work can have so much value. And how such a reserved and solitary man as Nogami Kenjirō can be so famous and respected throughout the country.

A week ago it was the Day of Culture, and a large celebration was organized in Mashiko to honour Nogami Kenjirō and other reputed artisans in the region.

Kenji was at the celebration. He also comes to see Simon regularly. They speak very little, but his presence comforts Simon. They often walk for hours in silence on the surrounding roads that wind throughout the countryside, segmented by the tiny cut-outs of cultivable land. They also help Nogami Kenjirō replace a few piles that are in poor condition, repair the sliding doors and chop wood — red pine — for his ovens.

On his last visit, Kenji brings Simon the mail he picked up from his apartment.

Geneviève has written to her father for the first time in her life. Simon doesn't even recognize her writing.

There are only a few words, scratched out in pencil on a lined sheet of paper that is torn from a notebook.

Simon,
    I passed all my courses during winter session and the fall session has started off well. Maybe I'm not a hopeless case like you think!

Geneviève
xxx

After reading the letter, Simon cries alone in his room.

During the three years after his divorce, Simon tried to re-create a bond with his daughter, away from Sophie. But nothing was the same anymore. Geneviève only came to see him every other weekend. Each time, they had to rebuild the bridge between them. Everything became more and more awkward and artificial.

Eventually, Simon gave up.

Geneviève did too.

When she was six, she decided that she wasn't going to go to her father's anymore and that her real family was in Westmount. Sophie had remarried and just had another child.

Geneviève didn't even want to go to restaurants or the movies with her father.

Simon didn't do anything to make it otherwise. Deep down, her decision made it easier for him. Now he was uncomfortable with Geneviève. He didn't know what to say to her anymore, or what she was interested in.

After that, at Christmas and on Geneviève's birthday, Simon took gifts to Westmount. Sophie invited him in to the living room each time, but he preferred to stay in the entry. Geneviève unwrapped her gifts on the floor and thanked him, intimidated, without even a kiss. Simon would leave immediately, relieved that it was over. He hated the visits.

It lasted seven years. The last two years, Geneviève wouldn't even be home when he went by, though they always agreed on a time.

For two years, Simon hadn't seen his daughter.

Then one Sunday, fourteen-year-old Geneviève arrived at Simon's apartment at five in the morning.

She had spent the night out, having a wild time downtown with her friends. She had been drinking and smoking.

If Geneviève hadn't said who she was over the intercom and he hadn't recognized her voice, Simon would have had trouble believing the adolescent standing at his door was his daughter.

For six months, Geneviève had been into the Gothic look. Her face was white as though it were bloodless. Her eyelids, lips and nails were painted in black, like her hair, which she'd dyed. She wore a large cape that smelled of the earth, as though she had been rolling on the ground. It was September 18 but you would have thought it was Halloween.

In the face of such an apparition and at such an ungodly hour, Simon's reflex was to ask Geneviève without the slightest panic if she had come from a masquerade party.

When he understood that for Geneviève this was not a costume, and that she had run away, he was swept up in a wave of panic.

Simon asked the woman in his bed to get dressed and leave.

Then he demanded that Geneviève explain herself. But she was in no state to do so. She went and locked herself in the bathroom to vomit. When she came back into the living room, she dropped onto the large sofa and fell asleep right away.

For nearly an hour, Simon paced furiously through the apartment, continually returning to Geneviève.

It hurt Simon to see all of the black on his daughter's body. He wanted to remove the grotesque makeup and clothing, wash her, powder her like he did when she was a baby, and put her in a tiny sleeper with feet, something that was clean and smelled good. He wished that she was little again so he could hold her against his shoulder and walk with her in this apartment where suddenly everything had become very worrisome.

Deep inside, Simon knew that he had abandoned Geneviève one day and that now she was floating back to him, as though she had drowned.

He would have liked to revive her, talk to her, pulverize all the silence that had solidified between them over the years. But he was at a complete loss, impotent. And he thought it was too late anyway. That the harm had been done and could not be undone. That the irreparable existed and it would do no good to try and undo the past. He knew from experience.

Simon was suffocating from his pain and definitely had to get a hold of himself before Geneviève resurfaced.

So he fell back on the only weapons he had to combat suffering, and he managed — painfully — through his own will to transform those unbearable feelings into logical, cold reasoning: Geneviève was in the middle of an adolescent rebellion.

That explained everything. He had nothing to do with what was happening to her.

And, when Geneviève awoke with her hangover and new manner — such a crude one at that — of expressing herself, the anguish that had gripped Simon was extinguished for good.

At eight o'clock, he called Sophie to tell her not to worry any more, that Geneviève was at his place. Sophie was totally over-whelmed by all the brutal changes that had taken place in her daughter in barely a few weeks. Several times during that period, Sophie had wanted to see Simon to discuss Geneviève. Each time he had refused and ended the conversation with a few peremptory statements, calling Sophie a mother hen and rigid conformist. In his opinion, this rebellion was healthy and was only meant to free the adolescent from her mother's suffocating grip.

During the years that followed, and until Geneviève's unexpected visit last December at Christmas, Simon had hidden behind the screen of these statements and hadn't been alarmed by the many changes in his daughter. But when he picked her up at the airport a few months ago, his lovely reasoning crumbled.

Geneviève had the unhealthy look of certain scrawny models. Her colour was pallid and her eyes dark. She barely ate at all to keep up the ethereal and sickly image that, more than anything she said, revealed all the devastation inside her. Her voice was dull and she didn't go to the trouble of finishing her thoughts. She only uttered scraps of sentences in reply to Simon's idle questions.

All the time that Geneviève was there, Simon felt pain like he had six years earlier watching her sleep in death's clothing on his sofa in Montréal. But Geneviève was going to be twenty in February. She was a big girl now. All her friends had finished their schooling, while she was still far from it. Simon could no longer rest on the fact that his daughter was having an adolescent rebellion to explain her worrisome marginality and strange behaviour.

Geneviève hadn't even told Simon she was coming. It was only once she arrived at the Tōkyō airport that she had called. It had taken her over six hours to reach her father by telephone. He could have been away for several days since it was getting close to Christmas. Simon didn't understand why she had taken such a risk. Nor why she had taken such a long trip when nothing in Tōkyō, or anywhere else in Japan, seemed to interest her. Often, she preferred to stay prostrate in his studio rather than go out. Simon had ended up admitting that she had probably come all this way just to be near him.

But the idea of this upset him so much he tried everything possible during the visit to distract her, hoping he could forget the cry for help she had come so far to emit for his ears only.

He could not.

They had both hurt for ten days, unable to say or do anything that reassured the other.

Then she left, at the beginning of January. And until he received her letter a few days ago, he didn't receive any news from her.

Yesterday, Simon wrote back to his daughter.

Geneviève,

I have never thought you were a hopeless case.

It's more that I thought I was one.

When you were born, the little girl that you were managed to break the armour I have worn since I was young to protect myself for fear of being hurt. For months, you awakened the best in me.

Yet one day I shut myself off brutally. And I fled far from you and your mother, hoping to turn back into stone and never feel again.

But your persistence and certain circumstances have pushed me out of my hiding place again. I am certain that it is for my own good, and yours too.

You don't have to risk your life anymore to reach me. Your father is back, for good.

Simon

EPILOGUE

The motley crowd of travellers has gradually spilled from the room and only the customs officers are left, waiting for stragglers or new arrivals.

Two suitcases from the last flight have been tirelessly making their way around the carousel for nearly an hour.

Behind the large glass walls, Chloé waits for the corporate man who has just burst through one of the automatic doors at the back of the customs area.

Simon picks up his heavy baggage. And then looks around for Chloé.

AFTERWORD

As Simon struggles to reconcile his past and present in the pages of *The Whole Man*, the theme of self-exile is woven intricately into the novel in several permutations — the theme of strangeness of the self and others at both individual and socio-cultural levels, of human struggle with past and present identity, and life in a foreign environment and an industry that alienate and isolate. The themes are provocative and raw in our modern times.

Simon is a consultant from a firm in Montréal, who works in Tōkyō. His working languages are Japanese and English, which is to say that Simon understands very little Japanese and his working language is English. Neither of them are his mother tongue, French. Simon, with his natural tendency to protect himself by isolating from others, thus places yet another degree between him and his immediate community. The existence of his translator, Kenji, is a human buffer who at once helps him function in Japan and keeps him on the outside of the culture, rarely having to speak Japanese. Simon is not at home in Japan and doesn't feel that he would be in Québec. He is told, "Then everything will gradually become strangely familiar, without him really noticing, even the language — the lilt of it will imperceptibly graft itself onto his. And one day, he will feel more like a foreigner at home than here."

Textual support is provided to this theme by the existence of Japanese and English words throughout the French text. Naturally, translation into English eliminates the visual contrast with the English words, meant to strengthen its presence between Japanese and Simon's mother tongue, French. In an attempt to compensate for the change, I have italicized the English words in the French text to indicate their foreign usage, and kept as much French in the English text as possible — leaving names of institutions, titles of address, and French words that are used in English in *The Whole Man*. Japanese words remain unchanged in the English; their existing diacritical marks are a significant addition to the theme of 'otherness'. I believe that, on the whole, this approach provides a plausible, thematic solution to the multilingual texture displayed in *L'homme au complet*.

Complementary to the multilingual text and concurrent with the theme of self-exile are the parallel story lines — Simon's past and present. Initially situated separately in time, they gradually converge as he reconciles his two lives. Simon's past is largely in the past and pluperfect tenses and, correspondingly, his present in the present and past tenses. As the novel progresses, this distinction wanes and eventually disappears. *The Whole Man* preserves the play between the two timelines, though some adjustments have been made for the sake of English readability.

The themes of *L'homme au complet* are extremely pertinent in these times. Aude's depiction of new, emerging virtual relationships between people and cultures is poignant and the depth of the character study is enthralling. It was a true pleasure for me to translate this work into English. I would like to thank the *Canada Council for the Arts*, *XYZ éditeur* and *Exile Editions* for their interest in this project. Special thanks go to Mara Bertelsen for translation discussion, input and encouragement and to Barry Callaghan for his great support.

Jill Cairns

MEMBER OF THE SCABRINI GROUP

Quebec, Canada
2000